ARMOR
OF
LIGHT

A NOVEL BY
ELLEN L. EKSTROM

WHYTE ROSE &
VIOLET, SCRIBES

ARMOR OF LIGHT

ISBN: 978-0615982380

Published in the United States of America

This is a work of fiction. Names, characters, places and
incidents either are the product of the author's
imagination or are used fictitiously and any
resemblance to actual persons, living or dead, business
establishments, events or locales is entirely coincidental.

Cover design: Whyte Rose & Violet Artists
Images courtesy of frizio (AI generated) at Adobe Stock
and Susan Stewart via iStockPhoto.com

WHYTE ROSE & VIOLET, SCRIBES
Berkeley, CA USA
www.whyteroseandviolet.net
admin@whyteroseandviolet.net

*For Celia, who is my strength
and armor of light. Thank you.*

ARMOR
OF
LIGHT

CHAPTER 1

For salvation is nearer to us now than
when we first believed. The night is far
gone, the day is near. Let us then lay aside
the works of darkness and put on the
armor of light.

Romans 13:11c-12

I f you've no money to spend, best get on."
Robert's breath was wasted. The young
stranger didn't move and was still looking, hands
on narrow hips, when Robert repeated himself in a
less than cordial tone. The stranger shook his head
and waved a hand at the shelves. There were plenty of
swords—enough to array the town guard—and the
price was good. There was something for every kind
of man at arms: broadswords, daggers, Robert had
them all.

The sun crossed the smithy while this young man
studied the cluttered shelves. Rays of winter sun
threw dusty shafts of light over a head of tousled,

golden hair that went from the brightest gold to burnished copper; they highlighted the dust and mud of a long journey on clothes that had seen better days. His cloak still showed signs of worth but it had been patched once too often and the back was faded, as if it had faced the sun for weeks. The white tabard beneath it was torn and rust-stained and on its breast, the crudely-repaired arm of a Crusader's cross was visible through a threadbare spot in the cloak.

"Did you not hear me, sir? If you've no money, you'd best—"

The stranger reached for the topmost shelf and pulled a fine sword from under a heap of lesser weapons. He hefted the sword, testing its weight, and tried a few moves so that the sun flashed off it in bursts and sparks. Figure eights, broad circles, and flourishes caught Robert's attention. He laid aside the polishing rag he'd been clutching in his fist and smoothed his leather apron as he came from behind the counter. Now that the stranger was an arm's length away and in better light, he looked much younger and nobler than Robert supposed. The face was tanned and unlined, and his large, blue eyes looked like they were made of quartz. He heard it said that eyes were the windows to the soul, but this young man's eyes were like mirrors. Robert could see his own face reflected back. There were no glimpses into his soul. There was something disturbingly familiar in the lad and Robert struggled to guess.

"I see you know the best, sir," Robert murmured. "That sword's never been used; it was made on commission by baron Waldric of Northumbria for Lord Thomas Fitzhugh's son, Oswin, when he was struck knight. I suppose you've heard of them?"

"Thomas Fitzhugh of Lichfield? I knew him. And his son. Oswin could never duck—neither in tilt yard nor on a field," the stranger remarked as he examined the sword. "He was best suited for chanting psalms, you know, and his father, well, more than once he had a squire waiting at the edge of a battlefield with a horse ready to ride. With Waldric following close behind, of course. I suppose that's why the sword is still here."

Robert snorted, and then laughed outright. "Bold enough words! You didn't know the Fitzhughs are great lords in these parts?"

"I know the cut of their cloth—though your words are bold indeed to make them so great."

"Well, if you knew them—"

"I knew enough of Oswin to know there wasn't much left of him after—how much?"

He tried the sword again, this time throwing it into the air and catching it. On the third round, Robert reached for the sword and grabbed it by the leather-bound grip, fearing the worst—that some harm would come to his best-made weapon in the hands of this foolish lad.

"If you have to ask you can't afford it. The silver and jewels in the pommel alone cost a gold angel!" Robert scoffed.

"How much for this? Would it be a fair exchange?"

The stranger unloosed the sword hanging from a sheath on his belt and offered it. Robert knew the sword—he'd made it almost thirty years ago and it looked all the worse for wear. The original leather and gold wire wrapping on the grip was replaced by rough cloth. There was a gaping hole where a large sapphire once sat in the pommel. The inscription along the blade's fuller was worn down from honing and sharpening so that only the 'A' and 'T' of the scripture sentence he'd engraved with patience and dedication was decipherable.

Robert took a step back, sputtering as if the breath had been squeezed out of him, and dropped to one knee. "George Ascalon! My lord of Grasmere! Pardon! I didn't know you—that is, I didn't know you'd come home; there've been stories going 'round about how you were put to death in Constantinople, so,"

"How much, sir? There's not a tradesman in Grasmere who'd turn away a sovereign or angel, even if it came from a dead man like me."

Robert dared to glance up. "Wha—?"

"I said, how much for my sword—in fair exchange?"

"That's the sword I made for your father when he was struck knight!"

"It's not doing him much good these days, is it?"

"You couldn't!"

"And who's to stop me?"

"Two angels, then!"

"Come, man! A sword like Fitzhugh's is worth at least five, and the sword of Ascalon has been valued at eight. I can give you six if it's a better profit you want."

"Begging your pardon, my lord, that's your father's sword," Robert said, nodding at the weapon in George's right hand. "Why on earth would you want to sell it for something less? Why at all?"

"I thought that would be apparent to all in Grasmere."

George Ascalon made ready to turn over his sword and paused, studying it. He glanced at the other for a longer moment and then carefully placed it back on the shelf. The sword of Ascalon went back into his scabbard. Robert made an exasperated sound, knowing he'd lost a sale that would thatch the roof and buy coal for the rest of the winter.

"Truly sir, I didn't know it was you; it's been a while, two, almost three years, hasn't it? It's been a long day—I wouldn't have been so cross; I beg you, take no offense!"

"None taken."

A golden angel flew out of the young man's palm and landed on the counter to spin wildly among swords laid out for repair. Robert snatched the precious coin before it sailed downward into the rushes.

"God speed," George called over his shoulder. He made ready to leave and then wheeled about. "Is the Golden Vine still at the end of Butcher's Lane?" he asked.

Robert nodded and came to the door, pointing the way up a lane flooded with the amber glow of a setting sun.

"Just beyond the glover's. You'll see the apothecary first."

"Then I know the way."

Robert nodded and watched the broad, straight back of the young man as he trod up the lane, waiting until he was a speck in a maze of wattle and daub cottages before slamming the shutters on the coming night.

The noise made George turn and look at the cottages and shops behind him. His eyes darted from dwelling to shop and back again, waiting. The shout for lights made him glance into the west. What caught his attention then was a formation of clouds over the lake. They drifted lazily together and finally met in one cohesive shape though it was hard to tell what the shape might be. First it was a boat, then a flower, and, at last, a beast of some kind. He paused a moment to study them and wheeled about, choosing to walk north toward Canterbury Street to a favorite haunt of past days, Deadman's Last.

Two and a half years had passed since he left Grasmere, yet all was the same. Every cottage and shed seemed to have been preserved in winter ice and snow, slumbering in the intervening days. This impression was never more so apparent than when George approached the inn and tentatively pushed the door open.

He sucked in a breath of foul, greasy air as he entered the common room, the same stale air he'd inhaled a thousand times before. If he were to go into the kitchen, he'd find Joan the scullery sleeping close by the coals of a dying fire. The meat would still be on the spit, dry and tough from turning all afternoon; the small beer would be flat. The bread, if there was any, would be stale or moldy. And the girls . . .

Ah, the girls.

The common room was filled with travelers stopping for the night and a few found spaces on the floor beside a hearth that belched clouds of smoke.

George glanced about and saw Will Draper, the weaver from Kettle Lane, sitting at a table by the kitchen door. Beside him, as always, was Stephen Black, the sheriff of Cumbria. Off in the corner beside the hearth was the only vacant table in the room with an empty trencher and cup laid out. A lamp over it glowed like a beacon. George made his way through the cluster of patrons and sat down at the table. When he raised the cup, a perfect, dark circle lay underneath. He took the lamp off its hook on the wall and set it on the table. From around his neck, he removed a leather satchel and emptied its contents before him: a Bible, icon, and a dark stone polished by age and water.

"It's true!" Ralf the innkeeper swore as he burst out of the kitchen. "I heard you'd been seen on the road from York!"

"How are you, Ralf?"

"Better than most these days. I suppose you'll have stories to tell, eh, my lord?"

"That would depend on who wants to hear them. Broth and bread, some meat—if it's fresh. Oh, and a clean bowl and cup?" Two gold coins fell out of the worn scrip tied to George's belt and he pushed them toward the man. "May I have the loft room? I'm not ready to go home."

"It's already yours! Welcome back, sir!"

The meal came quickly. George folded his hands before him and was ready to give thanks for the food when he noticed one of the patrons watching him with too much interest: an old gentleman who, in the dusky light and shadows, resembled a crow, the miserable birds that used to nest at his father's castle and torment George when he was a boy. George reached for the pot of ale instead and drank deep, wiping his mouth on the hem of his cloak.

"That's a Crusader's sword!"

George ignored the rather loud whisper at first, but that one whisper was joined by many. He turned to see that they came from travelers seated by the hearth: a youngish man who wore the cloak and cap of a scholar, a pale boy, the old crow, and several Lombard merchants. He gave them a look that warned silence and pushed bread across the trencher to sop up broth, took another drink of ale, and then filled his cup from the pot. These innocuous movements seemed to entertain, for George's audience kept staring as if there was nothing else to do but watch a man eat.

"He's been in the Holy Land!" the boy exclaimed. "I've seen those swords. Only Crusaders have them. Sir! Sir! Are you a knight of the Temple? A Templar?"

"You've a good eye, boy," George said between bites. "Now leave me to my supper."

"You didn't answer me. Are you or aren't you?" the boy demanded, coming close and standing over George. The roundness of the boy's still childlike face was made more apparent by the flickering lamplight. He looked no more than fifteen if that. His peat-colored hair cast ruddy highlights and his eyes, though wide for the moment, looked tired and dull. George knew he was of some consequence in the world, for when the boy opened his mouth his teeth were white, clean, and even. He stank of garlic and onions, not of decay.

"I suppose you killed a fair number of Saracens

with that?" the boy queried, reaching for the sword.

"I suppose," George answered. "It could kill a few more. Or a boy who won't leave be." George rested his fingers on the hilt and used them to gently remove the boy's hand. "Look you, sir, I've been a long way from home, and I want to finish my supper quietly. Surely you know from your betters how to leave be?"

"Master Adam, be quiet and sit down! Leave well enough alone!" his companion hissed.

"Let him speak!" the old crow rasped, heaving himself up on a fine walking staff carved with ancient symbols of the Old Ways. He limped forward and leaned heavily on the table, jostling George's pot of ale. Spilling the drink annoyed George; the old man's stare unnerved him. Nevertheless, George smiled and nodded in greeting, saying, "Is there something you want, old man?"

"Let the boy ask. Or maybe you don't want to talk of it. After all, there's no pride in coming home a coward."

"And who might you be, to pronounce my lot?" George demanded quietly.

"It doesn't matter who I am; all that really matters is what you're going to do," the man replied though George paid more attention to the velvet gown he wore than the words spoken. It fell in large folds over an emaciated frame, as if cut for a larger man, and the gold embroidery was tarnished from wear and age. Dull patches marked where jewels once decorated the fabric. Pushing the lamp towards him, George got a better look.

"I think I should know you," George murmured,

pulling the lamp back.

"You just might—"

"—I tell you again, my lady must have a room for the night! Not for herself, alone, mind; her maid has taken ill and must rest. It's too far a ride to Arkengarthdale! And tell this boy to let his betters by!"

The shout made George and his interrogators look toward the common room door where two travelers had their entry barred by the spit boy brandishing a metal rod upon which a partridge was skewered.

"Like my boy told you, there's no more room," Ralf interjected. "If the lady wants to stay the night, I can give her new straw and a good blanket. We can clear away the kitchen and the girl can rest there if she wants privacy. Or go to the abbey – they have an infirmary."

The man looked about nervously and leaned closer, saying in a low voice. "The girl is a Jewess! The abbey would never take us. You do understand?"

"Well enough!" Ralf stated, straightening his back. He jerked his head towards the door. "On your way!"

"A room! Do you know who her father is?"

"Her father could be John the blessed bloody Baptist and it wouldn't do her any good tonight! Not for you or your kind!"

"And what if the girl dies? What then?" the man shouted and silenced the room.

"It'd be one less serving girl, and I'm sure you'd find another before long," Ralf grumbled. He glanced behind them into the lane. "Where's this girl?

I see no lady's maid."

"The lady may take my lodgings," George spoke up.

The man glanced around the heads of the patrons to see who had spoken and nodded deferentially when George rose and came forward.

"George Ascalon, earl of Grasmere, sir," Ralf introduced. "And do you know who his father is?"

"Who does not?" the man gushed. "Sir, my lady and I are indebted to you for this small kindness!"

"Now just a moment!" Ralf protested. He turned to George, smiling nervously. "My lord, you cannot sleep in the common room! These people—"

"I'm sure their gold is as bright as mine, Ralf. Just see to it—for old times' sake if nothing else."

George now looked at the woman standing to one side, her face shadowed by a hood and the now dim light. He could see that she was fair of color and her eyes though smudged with the lack of sleep, looked bright enough, perhaps blue and perhaps slate. What he noticed most of all was the serenity. In the midst of chaos, she was calm and looked otherworldly.

George nodded in greeting. "No kindness is ever too small."

"I am Stephen Langley, steward of the Golden Tower." The man announced. "May I present Lady Richildis of Eskeleth?"

She threw back her hood, stepping forward into better light and looked directly at George. Although he'd loved or bedded a number of women, he'd swear an oath on twenty Bibles that none were as beautiful as this young lady.

George was fair of eyes and hair, but Richildis of

Eskeleth was fairer. What caught his attention more than her eyes was her hair. It was so pale gold it looked transparent. He imagined what it would be like with the sun streaming through it, and wondered if her pale skin was just as incandescent.

"Madam, you do me honor," George took her hand to kiss it. To his surprise, she withdrew her hand and enclosed it in the folds of her cloak.

"My thanks are in proportion to your offering, sir," she said, her voice soft, low, and musical. George now imagined how it would sound in song, perhaps a chanson de virelai. He was tempted to take the fantasy further, to a bedchamber in a castle somewhere in France, when the boy called Adam shoved his way into their circle.

"My lady, I have better quarters in a manor at Little Langdale. Why should you be given a bachelor's rooms? They're bound to be full of lice or vermin! I gladly offer the manor rooms leased to me, for it befits your station and beauty," Adam pronounced. He grinned boldly and made a sweeping gesture so that his hair almost dusted the floor when he bowed.

"Would you, indeed?" George murmured.

"Forgive the young man, Lady," the boy's companion hissed, "he is Adam Middleton, heir to the lordship of Gawthorp, and thinks his title gives him leave to speak whatever comes out of his mouth!"

"Most of it foolishness," said George. "His father would be ashamed to hear it."

Adam's dull eyes flared for a moment and he placed a hand on his sword hilt, being careful to show the lady he carried such a weapon. He turned to

George and offered a look of flint though he was forced to crane his neck, for George was taller than most men.

"Do you presume to know my father?" Adam demanded.

"I do. I fought beside him many times."

"Ah! Forgive me! You are the celebrated George Ascalon!" said Adam with a tinge of sarcasm and adolescent bravado. "My grandfather says you fled the taking of Constantinople, that you left your men to die by Byzantine swords and atrocities. How foolish was that? How did it feel, to take flight on a ship from Byzantium, getting away free and clear?" Adam continued, his voice and stance growing bolder.

"You are mistaken!" George hissed, trying hard to keep his temper. "Good night."

George pushed his way out of the common room. He let the door bang against him and waited there on the threshold to take in the stinging cold night air while he cooled his temper. He was deciding what to do next when he noticed two men and a girl approaching from the east, coming from the deserted market square. George wouldn't have given them a second thought until they were close enough for a look. The girl was covered in horrific sores that bled and oozed the worst of a body's impurities. Rather than shrink back, George met them at the door.

"I've seen this," George said, looking from one man to the other and then finally the girl.

"Have care! It's certain to be plague!" one of the men hissed as George touched the girl's forehead and found it as he expected – burning hot and damp with sweat. "She is past contagion. The worst is over if the sores rupture and fever takes her for a while, and that has happened. I've seen this in the Holy Land. Do not feed her but give her nothing more than water tonight. God keep her safe and you also, good men." Having said this, George bade them a good night and paused only for a moment when he noticed the lady Richildis, watching.

"Christ before me, Christ beside me, Christ above me, Christ below me."

Words from an ancient prayer came to his lips. George crossed himself and stepped out into the lane, walking toward St. Cuthbert's Abbey in the northeast part of town.

The streets were now quiet, save for a stray dog sniffing piles of midden and a wolf growling from a hiding place among the trees against the abbey walls. Yet George heard the unmistakable sound of boots and spurs on the path behind him. Gripping the hilt of his sword and closing the other hand around a dagger at his waist, George slowed his pace, straining to hear as the wind picked up. The footsteps quickened and George drew his sword, spinning a half circle to find a pale, diseased Crusader staring at him, the soldier's breath rising in noxious, billowing clouds from his mouth.

"Iou nteserb to nté phor iour sins!" the Crusader rasped, struggling for air and it was apparent why. His neck was covered in a torn, filthy and bloody bandage and a great wound was visible at the throat.

"What?" George demanded, taken off guard and unsure of what the man had said. His knowledge of Greek was excellent, but the words were meshed together, more like a cry in pain than a sentence.

"*Iou nteserb to ntê phor iour sins!*" he said again, then adding in French: "*Vous méritez de mourir pour vos péchés!*"

You deserve to die for your sins.

George understood now. He raised his sword and, with a shout, let it fall rapidly—on nothing

He looked about, puzzled, turning a full circle, listening but only hearing the wind in his ears and the soft padding of a dog as it hurried across the street to get out of George's way. The street was empty, quiet. Trembling from cold and confusion and some shame, he sheathed his sword and waited. When nothing unexpected or strange happened, George continued on towards the abbey. From time to time he glanced back and was glad to see no one.

The abbey's postern gate was unlatched, although it was past dark. The Benedictines of Grasmere were accommodating to travelers and thieves alike who passed in and out of the borderlands, paying no mind to their business or the hour. George glanced at the porter snoring on his bench and dropped a silver penny in his lap as he went by. He walked a familiar path among the vegetable and herb gardens, past the infirmary, to the abbey church. George went in and sat in one of the choir stalls, the wood groaning under his weight, and was there for some time when a door opened and fell shut, and footsteps echoed then stopped suddenly.

"*Benedicte*, friend: have you need of food or lodging—George? My blessed saints, is that you?"

George barely turned at the voice. He watched the candlelight dancing off the polychrome Virgin in her vestibule and then began whispering the prayer again, letting the words fall in their familiar pattern.

Christ before me, Christ beside me, Christ above me,
Christ below me, Christ behind me, Christ around me . . .

Footsteps clipped and echoed on the sandstone pavement, an uneven gait, grew close, and then stopped.

"It is you! I thought it was; I didn't want to hope—you've grown some. What a man you've become!"

George looked out into the shadows where the man stood. "How is it with you, Father?"

"Your mother told me she received a letter full of nonsense and rambling, how you quit crusade." A Benedictine brother materialized in the glow of a lantern and settled into the stall beside George's. "It's good to see you, Geordie!" After a painful silence full of innuendo, he reached up to tousle George's hair as if he was a small boy, but George grabbed the hand. A thin, white scar that looked like a tree branch spanned Aubrey Ascalon's palm and did not go unnoticed by his son.

"What's here? I don't remember this. Cut yourself making parchment for bibles?"

"An old battle wound," Aubrey explained.

George wrestled free and in doing so, the icon hanging around Aubrey's neck caught his attention. The image was visible in the candlelight—an enchanting and beautiful Madonna. George stopped the icon swaying in its course with a thumb and forefinger and studied it more closely.

"*Mater Dolorosa.* This used to hang over your bed. I've always wondered about the woman who posed for this. Is it Mother?"

"A woman important to no one except to God. A gift from one who was once a friend. How you stare at it! I'll not deny she was uncommonly beautiful . . ."

"Lady Jacopa from Florence or Elizabeth of Derwent? I lost count of your mistresses long ago," George remarked. He now glanced at the man sitting to his left. It was like looking into a still pond at his own reflection, he thought. The only difference was the span of twenty years that separated father and son.

"You're unhurt? No wounds?" Aubrey queried, holding the lantern close.

"None a man can see," George murmured, and then, "You've done well for yourself, Father. Lord Abbot, I hear. Some say you'll be Archbishop of York."

"Were I a favorite of the king, yes, but I have enough enemies and those whose anger will not be quelled barring any hopes of that."

"Mother."

"Exactly." A telling pause and then a sigh. "I suppose your mother hates me now."

"No more than any wife whose husband gives up all, exchanging one lord for another." The statement was just that, a statement; not a conviction, nor accusation.

"And you?"

"Doesn't matter what I think, does it?"

"Yet you returned."

"Not because of what you did. It's not important. I'm home."

"Much will be made of your return . . ."

"It's a foolish undertaking," George stated.

"Surely not what our Lord intended when He asked us to love one another!"

Aubrey leaned closer, gripping George's hand. "George, people are whispering evil things about you, of what happened in Constantinople, and there are stories—"

"I came home because I was sick of war and sick of watching people die, of killing men. Where is the dishonor in that? I came home because rather than let your lands and revenues fall to the king or his favorites, I want to claim them for myself, as is my right as your son if you must know. Besides, my sister and mother have no one to protect them."

"Not fair, George; not fair!"

"Was it fair when you left the note for Mother and said not even a word of goodbye, or gave a truthful explanation?"

"When the call comes it's one that you don't ignore or dismiss lightly. I'd pretended for so long."

"Ah, that would explain why you sent me off to murder in the name of Christ. You wanted someone else to do your dirty work while you prayed away the hours."

"You don't understand—or don't want to!"

George waved away further explanation. "Tell me this. Am I the earl of Grasmere, or did you sell my inheritance to purchase your holy orders?"

"Look there."

George glanced to where his father's elegant hand directed, a hand muscular and large that used to wield a sword and now held a prayer book. The hand's shadow fell on the smiling, docile Virgin.

"At the foot of the Virgin there is a loose paving

stone. Beneath that is the title and warrant for your lordship."

"Why do you hide it?" George wanted to know, rising up and taking a step. Aubrey held him back.

"Leave it. If anything should happen to you, your family is safe."

"Not our family, Father?"

"All is provided for; I saw to it, made sure it was done."

George was ready to argue and tell his father he was a fool for giving up an ancient birthright but the abbey bells struck the hour and Aubrey embraced him. "Come and see me again, George, for I have missed you!"

The familiar embrace made George's heart pound. The father he remembered, the gilt giant with merry blue eyes, the man who laughed and played with him, the man who rode to war as happily as tumbling his latest mistress in his great bed, was nowhere to be found in the pale contemplative now hurrying off to Chapter, leaving behind a scent of frankincense and a lifetime of regret. George waited for the footsteps to die before he left the abbey church. For the second time that day he would leave a familiar place with a heavy heart.

Out beyond the postern gate, George pulled his worn cloak about him to stave off the wind that now brought a light snowfall. He stamped his feet against the cold and tried to decide which way to go—back to the inn or on to Skelwith Castle, his family's home at Little Langdale. Looking to the west, he saw the reddish glow on the horizon and frowned. The tang of burning wood and fiber filled his nostrils as a new wind assailed him. A house in the poor neighborhood of Butcher's Lane had gone up.

George sprinted to the market square and rang the bell, then headed towards the conflagration.

CHAPTER 2

A HALF-DOZEN men stood in Butcher's Lane watching as a thatched-roof cottage lit the sky like a monstrous torch. A few drank from leather skins and laughed and cheered as if it was a bear baiting or a mummer's show, especially when a woman's screams rose over the groan and roar of timber crashing. When George made for the cottage, two of the onlookers held him back.

"Leave off, sir!" one man growled. "It's better this way!"

"You can't stand by and let it burn! Someone's in there!" George protested, struggling. "Leave off, I said! Let go of me! You don't know who I am!"

"Someone who should leave well enough alone!" growled a priest who stepped out of the crowd.

"I am George Ascalon, earl of Grasmere!" George shouted and he reached for his sword. His captors released him when they saw the medallion of the earls of Grasmere around his neck.

Now free, George sprinted toward the house. He tore off his cloak and dragged it through a snow bank until it was sodden, then wrapped himself in it. Holding the hems to his mouth and nose, he crouched and entered.

Ghostly shapes wavered in the orange light of dancing flames. One of them was a woman huddled beside the only window. George crawled over to her and with a free hand grabbed her arm, pulling her towards the door. To his surprise, she refused to move.

"Save yourself!" the woman cried.

"You can't stay here to die!" George shouted. "You can't stay here! Come with me!"

"Leave me! It's what they want! It's what he wants!"

George ignored her protests and dragged her out, skirting timbers crashing down around them, avoiding new pockets of flame as the cottage was consumed in what became an inferno. They both collapsed in the lane a safe distance from the cottage, heaving and gasping for air. Scooping up a handful of new snow, George offered it to the woman, who was no woman at all, but a girl. She wiped her face with the snow as she coughed, expelling black soot from her mouth and lungs.

The girl sat up and let out a scream, then started to keen and choke back wretched sobs. The cottage collapsed and a new burst of flames shot up into the sky, devouring what was left of the timber and wattle.

"It's gone!" the girl wailed. "He'll blame me! You should have left me to die!"

"You had no business!" the priest spat, coming to stand over them. "You interfered with God's work!"

"Strange work God does, to let a girl burn to death in a cottage," George snapped back, getting to his feet and pulling the girl with him.

"She's a witch!" said the priest.

"And how do you know that?"

"The mark of the devil on her arm!" he said,

pointing at her sleeve.

"I am not!" the girl cried and then looked to George. "Truly sir, I am no witch!"

"She has the mark!" the priest insisted. "I've seen it myself! It changes color, from purple to blue, to green and yellow!"

"It's no mark of the devil! The man who keeps me locked up did this!"

The girl rolled up her chemise sleeve and revealed an ugly welt of reds and purples, greens and yellows that covered most of her forearm almost to the shoulder. The men gasped and stepped back cautiously as if waiting for something else. George brought the girl into better light and looked at the arm.

"It's the mark of a cruel beating, and more than one, I guess! Your man did this?" George wanted to know, gently replacing the sleeve.

"Yes; I angered him—but I'm not his. He's not my man; I was married to a fletcher of Salop but he died, and so I came here."

She began to shiver then, the cold displacing shock, and she pulled her drab brown surcote about her small frame, trying to keep warm.

"No one deserves such punishment," George said quietly. "Where is he?"

"Sir, I beg you, leave me alone. If he finds out—I should have died in there. Living would be worse than death!"

"From this moment you are under the protection of the earl of Grasmere. You'll be a lady's maid to the countess, or a cook, or whatever she decides. Let this fool come to me and settle his quarrel," George said.

The girl wiped her nose with her sleeve and looked at him with wide, round, eyes. "You're a bold dog to speak so freely about what the earl of Grasmere would do!" she scoffed. "I've heard promises from men like you before!"

"Not from the likes of me."

"And what's like you?"

"Well, the earl of Grasmere, for one. And the lord of Skelwith Castle, too."

"Does the earl think the same?"

"I do hope so," George replied as he removed his sodden, steaming cloak and offered it to her. "I'm the earl—of Grasmere, for one; and lord of Skelwith Castle, too."

"Indeed you are!" the girl muttered.

"Kneel and give your courtesy!" hissed one of the men, pushing the girl to her knees.

"Why should I?" the girl argued and she struggled to stand, surprising the men with her strength and boldness. "Just because he says he's the earl of Grasmere and lord of Skelwith?"

"My lord of Grasmere!"

Stephen Black's voice caused the spectators to disperse quickly, hurrying out of the sheriff's sight as he approached George. A few men took respectful steps back and bowed their heads. "Sweet Gesu!" the girl muttered.

"Stupid whore!" the priest growled and grabbed her by the hair, pulling her down into the snow with such force that the girl began to whimper.

"Enough!" George shouted at the men. "Let go of her. Grasmere does not demand ceremony," he instructed, helping her up. He added, smiling at the girl, "Though simple courtesy would not be disregarded."

"You have no right to interfere, my lord!" the priest continued to whine; "She has the mark of the devil himself—"

George now whirled about, his sword out of its sheath. "You have the devil in your black heart! As I said, it's strange work God does to punish an innocent."

"She's no innocent!" the priest sneered. "You can ask any man in Butcher's Lane!"

"Or maybe I should question you further?" George growled back. "Unless you have a warm, safe bed and supper for this lady, you ought to mind your own business!"

"My lord!" Stephen Black said in greeting when he finally joined what was left of the crowd. "Is there anything I can do to help?"

"All has been seen to, Sheriff," George said nonchalantly. "God speed you a safe and warm night."

"Sir, you are mistaken in me—make no more of this," the girl whined as George led her out of the crowd and towards Deadman's Last.

"I've made an end of it. Now come with me."

"No, you haven't! And what about me? One moment I'm the whore of Butcher's Lane, the next an innocent,"

"Are you now?"

"No!"

"Innocent or whore, which is it?"

"Neither, I swear!"

"Well then?"

"Now it will be said I'm the companion of Grasmere!"

"Given your choices, would that be so terrible?"

"The earl of Grasmere and lord of Skelwith now thinks he knows my choices in life!"

"Thanks would be sufficient."

"Pardon?"

"I can understand why your man beat you!" George commented under his breath but loud enough for her to hear.

"You're no better than the rest of them! Did I not tell you, sir, that he is not my man? I am not his goods or chattel!"

"You whine and complain, yet not a word of thanks."

"Thank you, my lord of Grasmere," the girl said, trying to keep up with George's long strides. "I humbly beg your pardon. I am ever in your debt and beholden to your charity. I'm unused to such kind treatment and am an unworthy maiden. Will that do, my lord? Is that humility sufficient? Where are you taking me?"

"For a Butcher's Lane wench, you have your airs!"

They were at Deadman's Last. The stable boy snapped to attention when George appeared out of the snow. "The witch!" the boy gasped and crossed himself when he saw the girl hurrying to keep up with George.

"Any more talk like that and I'll give you such a hiding you'll wish you had magic to cure your backside! Get my horse. The roan with the white star on her forehead."

"Yes, my lord Grasmere!" the boy said and he ran to do George's bidding.

"A silver penny if you bring a loaf of bread and some meat! My lady is no doubt hungry. And find a cloak for her!" George called after him, and then turned when he heard the soft thump, thinking the girl had fallen. She was on her knees, head bowed. "What's this?" he asked.

"My thanks for your chivalry. That you should show such kindness..."

"Get up, if you please; no one here about kneels to the earls of Grasmere—not like they used to, or should," George said good-naturedly.

"I often forget that things are not what they were. I forget myself. Sometimes what I expect is not that to which I've been accustomed . . . it disappoints, you see."

George was going to ask what she meant when the stable boy returned, leading a fine mare and carrying a sack bulging with food.

"I assume you truly have nowhere to go?" he questioned the girl.

"Why should that concern you? Besides, you saw my home destroyed by fire." A moment passed, and then: "Ah, I see. You want to take back your promise."

"My word has no currency hereabouts, but I want to make restitution to one of my people. You are my responsibility."

"Why? It didn't concern the last earl of Grasmere."

"I assure you, I'm not that man," George answered quietly, meeting her gaze. She looked away first. "We'll ride to Skelwith Castle. You'll be safe there," he said after a time.

The girl balked. "Please, my lord, I cannot stay the night in the castle; it will be said—sir, you know what will be said. And the man who keeps me locked up—"

"The one thing you must do tonight is get yourself as far away as you can from this man who loves you so much he wounds you with kindness," George said, mounting up. "And what is your name? Do you have one?"

"Joanna. Joanna Fletcher. My kinsmen and boon companions call me Joan."

"Well, Joanna, up into the saddle with you."

He waited while the girl fumbled for the stirrup and then swung easily into the saddle. "Sir, I beg of you, take me to a convent if there's one nearby. Otherwise, it will be said—"

"It will be said that George Ascalon is acting foolishly again, and it's nothing I haven't heard before," he answered, settling in front of her.

"It will be said you carried off a lady for your own sport!"

"Again, it will be said," George chuckled, turning to look at her. She was glaring at him. "A lady you say?" George queried. "Where do you get these notions?"

"Not a notion, sir, but a fact! The gossips in Cumbria are far worse than those in London!"

"Enough, Joanna!" George sighed as they rode off. "Count the stars or the sheep in the pasture, but quietly and to yourself!"

In between the clopping of the horseshoes on the

stones, George tried not to laugh as he heard a small voice behind him.

"One, two, three . . ."

✠✠✠

THE SKY WAS the color of pitch and the air had a tang of good, damp earth as George cantered up the approach to Skelwith Castle. He felt Joan slump against him and knew she had nodded off, slowing so that the horse's canter wouldn't rouse her. A signal went up from Ravenglass Tower, then another from the great tower of the donjon. Lights began to appear in the windows as word spread that George had arrived. He waited at the gate as the drawbridge lumbered down.

The great Norman castle of the earls of Grasmere had been built one hundred and thirty-nine years before by Ranulf Ascalon, who came over with the Conqueror. The formidable and beautiful keep of red sandstone stood on a hill on the outskirts of the village of Little Langdale, facing Windermere. This was George's birthplace and a place for which he had no happy memories. But it was something he had not enjoyed for a long while: a home and familiar surroundings.

He felt the shock of a breeze as Joanna stirred, her movements dislodging the cloak they shared. "Good evening, Mistress," George said. "Have a good sleep?"

"Marvelous . . ." she purred dreamily. George felt her tense as she said in a colorless, formal voice, "Pardon, sir, but where are we?"

"We're home," he said gently.

Servants came from the donjon with torches to

light the way. George dug rowels in and thundered across the bridge and into the greater bailey, saluting the watch in the guardhouse as he went past. His arrival brought a pack of hounds from around the corner of the stables, a stout groom in pursuit shouting curses at them and tugging at his cap when he saw George bounding out of the saddle.

"They never could mind, eh, Jack?" George laughed and was ready to join in the chase when a tall, imperious woman came down the steep casement from the donjon as if she were gliding on air, her coif flashing its jewels in the uneasy light of cresset lamps while the veils danced in a breeze. A bright bouquet of ladies-in-waiting hurried to keep up.

"This must be the countess," Joanna murmured as she slid off the saddle and stood beside George, the only familiar person in the small crowd gathering.

"Worse than that!" whispered George as the lady approached. He stepped up and met her halfway through the bailey. "Elinor! It is good to be home."

"Be it God's will and not ours," the woman murmured, and she offered a neat curtsy. Rising, her eyes fell on Joanna. "And who's this? A Saracen bride, my lord?"

Joanna fell awkwardly to her knees before the lady. In fact, she had tripped and was struggling to rise when George held a hand to her shoulder to keep her down as he said, "I've brought a new companion for my mother. Her name is Joanna Fletcher. I took her from a burning house in Grasmere this night. She had nowhere else to go—her man abused her and left her to die," George explained. "Mistress Fletcher, may I present to you my childhood friend Elinor

Lucy, daughter of the baron of Reeth, and the good and loyal wife of our chancellor, Sir William Longleate. Elinor, this is Joanna Fletcher."

Elinor assessed the girl before her with a dismissive glance and then gave all her attention to George, who was smiling. "Ah, my lord! What will your mother say? Your charity is puzzling yet obvious. Another leman for Grasmere?"

"Have care, lady, for this woman was defenseless in a situation both unjust and evil," George said low.

Elinor raised her brows at him, and said, "How do you know she's defenseless? Maybe she struck the flint!"

"I have forgotten myself—I've been away so long that I cannot remember who is master of this place. And perhaps so have you, Elinor?"

"You are what you are, my lord—just ask any woman in the castle."

Joanna reached out from where she knelt and tugged at the hem of George's tunic. He glanced down, frowning, but softened when he saw the fist clutching his hems. "What is it, Joanna?"

"You speak as if I weren't here, kneeling in the mud," the girl murmured unhappily. "Let me up, please!"

George motioned to the girl, who rose and offered him a sweet smile, one of gratitude, but he was glaring at Elinor. "Mistress Longleate," he said; take our friend Joanna to the ladies' bower and with all courtesy as would befit any guest in this castle. Let this be an end to our conversation."

"Be it as you will, my lord," Elinor answered with a neat curtsy of her own. "What's one more to this great household? Come, mistress; let us first go in to chapel and offer a prayer of thanksgiving for our good lord of Grasmere's charity."

"I'm not wanting charity," Joanna spoke up.

Elinor turned on her, eyes like flint and mouth set. "Others will think to the contrary, Mistress."

"I think—I think it would behoove you to beg your good lord's forgiveness. He doesn't deserve your anger or disapproval, not on my account."

"We shall have to keep you occupied, I'm sure of that—quick minds shouldn't be idle!" Elinor purred. To George she said, "Will that satisfy you, my lord?"

Rather than reply George threw her a glare and then led the way up the stairs and through the covered walkway inside, past the guards and servants, avoiding the hounds still barking and getting underfoot. While George greeted the knights, courtiers and servants assembled to welcome him home, he noticed Joanna's absence.

"Mistress Fletcher, will you not join us?"

Joanna was rooted at the threshold of the hall, head down and smoothing her dirty gown with hands no less unclean. In the brightness of the torches and candlelight, the night's misadventure was very apparent. Between patches of dirt and soot, the girl's skin was visible. Her gown, which looked to be a saffron color and had once been costly, was torn, daubed with blood and dirt, stained in mottled shades of brown and green, and hung in limp folds over her tiny frame. She looked very much alone and unhappy.

"Would you like a bath?" George asked.

The girl's eyes darted upward and she looked panicked.

"Forgive me, Lady, tact is not one of my virtues," George apologized. "It was an innocent enough offer. Elinor, have a bath drawn and find her some clothes."

"So now I'm a wet nurse, my lord?" the lady snapped.

"I missed your kindness and the fetching way you endear yourself to others," George said to her. "Just do as you're bid, Elinor."

Taking the girl's hand, Elinor pulled her along to the north side of the great hall, moving toward the screen and muttering under her breath in the Welsh tongue, most of which was unkind and directed at George. Her anger was fueled when Joanna replied to her comment in flawless Welsh. "You dare!" Elinor hissed and boxed the girl on the ears.

"Damn you! You cow!" Joanna shouted.

"Elinor! Enough!" George shouted and all eyes fell on the women. For a moment it looked as if Elinor would continue the argument, but she merely raised her chin and tilted her head in question. George waited and then said quietly in close-clipped words, "Bring Mistress Fletcher to the bower and see that all is done as I command."

Joanna muttered her thanks to George and shot him a fleeting glance that cried "Help me!" as Elinor dragged her away.

Retainers and servants engaged themselves in banter and nervous conversation and all avoided George's gaze. He made no excuse for himself and walked toward the opposite end of the hall where a heavy curtain separated the hall and a staircase that led to 'The Lady Tower,' the countess of Grasmere's residence. George pushed aside the curtain and passed through, skipping two steps at a time until he reached the bedchamber doors. He paused a moment before turning the latch and slipped in quietly, falling to his knees before a diminutive woman seated at a window, a Bible in her lap.

"Mother?" George spoke up.

The Bible was slammed shut and Maud Ascalon looked at her son with a critical eye. "So! You're home." She took a folded square of parchment from inside the cuff of her sleeve, a square softened and creased from much handling. The ink of the address was faded and smudged. Maud held it out. "You would do well to explain this."

It was a moment before he spoke. "Everything I wrote was true. I make no excuses," George said quietly.

"Why come home, then? You might have gone straight to Jerusalem."

"Father has already taken holy orders; I didn't think you'd want to lose your only son to the church."

Maud struck him soundly across the cheek and yet George didn't flinch. "Forgiveness!" she hissed; "You would go to Jerusalem to be shrived!"

"One doesn't need to travel across the world to seek absolution."

"And you would return to face scorn and conjecture? You would stop your ears to what is being said?"

"It's no different than when I left Cumbria," George answered. He fumbled with the drawstring to his scrip and took from it a piece of jewelry—a Roman cross with five rubies glowing from their setting of hammered silver. "Perhaps this will lessen your pain, Mother? A gift from your brother Raymond—to remember him, should he not return."

"If this is from the plunder of Constantinople, keep it!" Maud ordered, handing back the cross.

"I shall offer it to the abbey—for alms. Perhaps it is one deed that you will approve of."

"God forbid that you—that my brother—I shall pray for him." She reached out and forced George to look at her, turning his chin with an icy hand. "I've not heard a word that I like or take comfort in, George."

"Knowing how much I hated taking up crusade, why would you think I took any pleasure in it?" he demanded.

"Other than women and drink, what pleasure do you find in life? How long will it be before we hear new stories and gossip, I wonder?"

"It's already started." George pushed himself to his feet, and in doing so, tucked the cross back into the scrip. As George prepared to leave, Maud took his hand. For a moment, he thought she would embrace him, but wasn't surprised by what happened next. "I've always regretted that your father never took a stick to your back," Maud sighed.

"He punished me in other ways," he answered. "As have you. I only wonder when you'll both stop blaming me for everything in your lives that's been a disappointment."

Opening her Bible, Maud let an elegant finger slide down the illuminated page as she followed the text. George couldn't help but notice that she had opened it to the parable of the Prodigal Son. She wouldn't utter the last word, but George knew from other contests that the last word was always hers, just by the way she opened up the Bible that was always within reach. Tomorrow they would recount this conversation in other words, but it would always end the same way.

As he had done so many times before, George retraced his steps to the donjon and the earl's apartments—but not in search of his father. He would go to claim the rooms as his own. He was at the spiraling staircase when Elinor came out of a chamber and blocked his path.

"My lord," she greeted with a curtsy. "Your friend is being looked after by your sister's women."

"That wasn't so hard a task, was it? My thanks, Elinor."

"The girl kept insisting she was a lady when I suggested she help the cook to earn her keep."

George smiled, saying, "We all pretend airs at one time or another to impress our betters or shield ourselves from hurt."

"You taught us well in that, my lord."

"I had my first lesson from you, Elinor. Good night."

When George made for the staircase, Elinor shifted slightly, making it impossible to move. "Imagine our surprise when we heard you were alive," she said. "We all thought you had perished in Venice, or in the fighting at Constantinople. When word came from—" Elinor was cut off by an unexpected kiss from George.

"What? No scolding? I flatter myself thinking that you missed me!" George whispered, and kissed her more deeply now.

She broke away saying, "I hoped you wouldn't return—I couldn't forgive you for what you'd done."

"Let me make amends."

George kissed her neck and gently pushed the neckline of her gown off her shoulders and now sought the naked skin that glowed under the dim torchlight. She relaxed in his arms and let his kisses wander, allowing his hands more liberties as they tugged at the precious silk fabric of her gown. George pulled her up the staircase towards the bedchamber, but they made it only as far as a window seat on the first floor, behind a curtain. Here they groped and struggled to kiss under layers of clothing, as longing led to urgency and finally release. George slumped against Elinor, who lay beneath him, her half-naked body draped in her own clothing and the curtain. When he opened his eyes Elinor was studying him, her handsome face set in a scowl.

"Let that be an end to us, my lord. We both know it can be no other way," Elinor said as she prevented George from kissing her again.

"You know why I left, Elinor; there was no other choice."

"What did you prove? That you have no stomach for war? Just as you had no stomach for being a lord, for being a knight, for being anything more than what you are?"

"You found solace with a good marriage and a good man."

"But he wasn't what your father promised me."

"He broke a lot of promises, Elinor, and not only to you."

"Nothing stopped you from proving him wrong."

He was going to speak, but instead, George arranged his clothing and smoothed back his hair, then offered Elinor a sterile kiss on the cheek.

"Goodbye, Elinor; some day when you're not so angry, perhaps you'll tell me why a lack of worldly ambition offends you so, and why I have to constantly prove myself to you."

Elinor's tirade grew fainter as he climbed the steps two at a time to the landing, and then three steps down to the solar door. She was an unpleasant afterthought when George unlocked the door and entered the earl's apartments.

Someone had kept the rooms spotless as if waiting for Aubrey's return. Even his harness and mailed shirt were oiled and ready to be worn, hanging from their willow-worked stand. His father's favorite tunic and shirt were laid out on the bed. A window was open, allowing the good, clean air of Cumbria to overtake the staleness of disuse. George sat on the bed and glanced about, half expecting his father to enter and throw his sword and spurs on the great table beside the wall hearth. There was movement at the door, but it was only one of the hounds, an old bitch that recognized George and lapped at his outstretched hand with a rough tongue.

Leaning against the plump bolster and holding his father's tunic, George closed his eyes for a moment and felt the warmth and sting of tears under the lashes. With the tears came memories of earlier days, when he and Elinor were playmates, then lovers, and then separated when he was forced to take up crusade in his father's stead. He never expected to be away so long, nor hold affection for her. Why should her reaction to his homecoming and the disdain that came with it be any more surprising than his ability to have survived Constantinople?

The journey from the east had finally taken its price of him. George felt an exhaustion he'd never felt before. He closed his eyes, and soon his dreams took a familiar turn. Like so many nights before, he was dreaming of soldiers storming the cathedral in Constantinople, of priceless gold vessels and jewels shoved at him by his uncle Raymond while men laughed and cheered; he could smell the exotic spices and incense, burning wood and flesh, as centuries-old buildings and treasures beyond belief were sacked and left in ruin; he could see the small child sitting in the courtyard of the house where he had lived and the soldiers coming for him. George was once again sprinting through the courtyard, where he picked up the child and ran for his life.

CHAPTER 3

O H, LORD! HERE he is! Do you think he's
dead?"
"Sleeping, not dead, my lady—my lord?
My lord? George?"

George felt the hand on his shoulder and tried to
bat it away. He felt the shakes and prodding and
opened his eyes to find a hideous face with glowing
red eyes staring at him, the air around him full of
sulfur, and the sky bright with flame. George
struggled to stand and grab for a sword that wasn't
there, ready to attack.

"Easily! Easy there, my lord!" Will exclaimed.
"Perhaps it was a bad dream?"

"George, are you well? What's amiss?" asked
Maud.

"It's nothing—what time is it?" he demanded,
sinking back onto the bed.

"What care should you have for the hour?"

"I said, what time is it!"

"Compline, at most, but why—"

"His mother said she would return, and then it
was too late; the Venetians came and it was too late . .
." George's voice trailed and he turned from them
and pressed himself against the bolster as if he wanted
to hide, curling up into a defensive ball. He began to
convulse and William did his best to calm him.

"I've seen this sickness in men who survived battle. It comes and goes in spells and in time it disappears altogether. Sleep is the best cure," Will said as he tried to pull back the covers and was prevented by Maud's icy grip on his arm.

"No, not here!" Maud ordered. "Let him have his old rooms." She motioned to Will. "Why do you tarry? Bring him to his feet and follow me!"

"I don't see why, my lady; it's just as well he sleeps here," Will grumbled. He struggled to get the larger man on his feet.

"Don't you know, Will?" George scoffed. "We mustn't disturb the earl's bedchamber— he might return at any moment! Truth be told, I'm the earl now, not my sainted father!"

Maud struck him across the face with such force that both men stumbled against her. She pushed them off and led the way in another direction to the largest of the towers in the outer curtain of Skelwith, to Ravenglass Tower, up a short flight to apartments set away from the rest. Selecting a key from the girdle at her waist, Maud turned the lock with some difficulty and then pushed open the heavy oak door. "Come through," she ordered and moved aside so that they could enter the cobweb-decorated antechamber and go through to the main apartments, disturbing dust and mice as they went. The difference between the earl's private apartments and his son's was disturbing. Nothing had been touched in the years George had been gone, even the shirt he'd thrown to the floor was still there. The wine-colored tunic his father had given him as a birthday gift was still wrapped with a silk ribbon and lay on a bench near the cold fireplace.

His beloved chess game was set on a table under the window, the pieces standing where they were left in the middle of a match. All were as he left it.

George coughed and put a hand to his mouth and nose, glancing about with disgust. He glared at his mother, who said in a dull voice, "We weren't expecting you to return."

"How heartwarming!" he muttered. George waved them off and against Maud's protests, threw himself on the unmade bed, ignoring the cloud of dust his movements caused and pulled the coverlet and blankets over him. "Take your leave," he growled from his sanctuary.

When he heard the door close, he reached under the bolster and found a scrap of cloth, a pale violet length of wool and held it close, his friend from a not too distant childhood. It still held the scents of rose and sandalwood, and they lulled him back into sleep—this time comforting and restful.

✠✠✠

LAUGHTER AND SINGING woke George the next day. He blinked in the bright sunlight warming the room and glanced at the candle, raising his brows when he saw that he had slept past noon—something he'd never done before. Throwing off the blankets, George rose and went to the window overlooking the lodge in the greater courtyard. The women of the household were seated at their needlework, and they sang while another girl played a harp. He recognized all of the women save one—a girl in a blue gown and whose features were obscured by dark hair and a silk veil, a girl with a perfect form, though small in proportion. She seemed to be the center of attention, for even Elinor was subdued in her presence.

One of the ladies-in-waiting saw George in the window and hailed a greeting. The rest of the women stood and bowed, waves of silk and wool, velvets and linen in different color rippling as they dipped gracefully—all but the dark-haired girl, whose head was bent over her work and whose needle flashed in the sunlight. Her indifference, if anything, intrigued George.

He hurried to shave and change his clothes, being careful to choose his best shirt and tunic, the finest girdle, splashing rosewater and sandalwood over his face, but by the time he bounded into the lodge, the women had gone inside. He was on their trail when William appeared in the doorway of the treasury.

"You look well, my lord," William greeted.

"Due in most part to the good climate and people of home," George responded, starting out again.

"Would you like to review the early accounts?"

"Another time, Will," George said, distracted because he had seen the ladies on the wooden bridge to the Lady Tower.

"I've spent a good part of the morning seeing that all of the books are in order. His grace your father would make it his first business of the day."

"Yes, yes," George said impatiently. "But I am a man who trusts, Will; and though it be said I am a poor judge of character, I am worse with numbers, and I trust your skill in ciphering. The household prospers."

"My lord!"

Elinor's shout was a portend of certain trouble. She glided down the steps of the donjon and made a path through the knights of the household gathering for inspection and scared away the children and dogs, as she approached. George grabbed Will's arm. "On second thought, I'll see those books," he said and steered Will back into the treasury. He didn't relax until Will shut the door behind them.

"If you would permit me, my lord," Will sighed as he sat across from George at a desk and pulled the account ledger towards them; "let me speak my mind about something that has bothered me these past two years. It would be best for all concerned."

"Granted," George said uneasily and thought, now it will come!

"I was ready to marry Lady Alix de Beaumont when your father arranged the marriage between Elinor and me. There was little I could do. She was Grasmere's ward and I won't deny that her portion was inviting, as was the lady herself,"

"Will, I never thought . . ."

"I never meant to take her from you, and well, my lord, here I do ask your forgiveness."

"It is given most gladly, Will. May you have many more years of her wit and charm and that her bower is inviting."

Will stopped a laugh and winked at George. He took a drink and then pointed to an open page in the ledger. "Ah! Here, my lord, you'll see that your idea of raising sheep and selling the wool has made a substantial profit."

"Indeed? I thought my father called it nonsense!"

"Of the best kind sir! We can go to the croft at Little Langdale and you may inspect the herd. Lombard merchants have purchased much of this year's wool."

"At least that's one idea of mine that came to fruition and failed to harm," George said as he ran a finger down a column, not daring to meet his gaze. "And here I do swear to you, my friend, that I will amend my life, and make reparation to you and all I've hurt." He looked over and saw the cup of wine extended. Taking it, he drank with Will and they continued to review the household accounts and talk about days long past, when Will came to the castle to learn knighthood, helped George take his first steps, came with him to fish in the lake at Grasmere, stood silently by when Elinor sought revenge on Will's indiscretion with a lady of the court by carrying on an affair with George soon after her marriage to Will, an affair that was the undoing of many.

"If you don't mind my asking, sir, why did you return? You could have gone to London and secured a place at court, or you could have gone to York or Paris," Will queried.

"Because I knew I could," George answered after a time. "And I suppose that is true of everything I've ever done—I did things because I knew I could."

After another cup of wine, the subject changed from past follies to grand dreams of the future, and George would have been content to stay and talk with Will if the business of running a lord's estate hadn't interfered. While Will went to investigate the latest crisis in the barley fields, George wandered about his castle with nothing to do. He eventually wandered up to the Lady Tower and slipped into the solar unnoticed, discovering a hive of activity in the usually quiet apartment.

Elinor was seated in a chair, reading aloud to the smaller girls in the household; Maud was offering praise to a young girl plying a needle expertly to a linen canvas upon which flowers were starting to bloom in glowing silk threads. The girl was extraordinarily pretty and her great mass of glossy hair was pulled back with ribbons, coils of hair as black as the finest Whitby jet with auburn streaks where the sun had turned it. Her dress was a deep shade of blue, shimmering with embroidered gold stars and as iridescent as the midday sun on a pond.

Strolling forward, smoothing back his hair and straightening his tunic, George stopped short when he realized the fetching girl who had caught his eye was Joanna.

All of the ladies glanced up and then got to their feet when George lurched to a halt and stumbled into a prie-dieu, knocking a Bible onto the floor.

"S-Sorry!" George stammered, never taking his eyes from Joanna.

"Well, you've not changed a bit!"

George turned and saw his sister Petronelle perched like a bright bird on the high window seat. Her plumage was luminous velvet and silk, striking shades of red and orange that showed her pale prettiness to full advantage. A heavy golden braid fell over a shoulder and was bound by ribbons and pearls. As George came forward for a kiss, he noted the betrothal ring, an obscenely large sapphire set in a golden band, weighing down the hand that held a prayer book.

"And neither have you—but I see some poor fellow decided he was more interested in the

Grasmere honors than having a beauty in his bed and at board!" George quipped and caught her hand in mid-air as she squealed in mock horror. He kissed it affectionately. "Who's the lucky man, Petra?"

"The earl of Chester," she replied, a pretty blush washing over her cheeks.

"Gesu! Did Mother have to enfeoff the manor at Grasmere to pay your dowry? I heard Chester turned down one of King John's bastard daughters for lack of a price!"

"No, I did not," Maud said. "John of Chester thinks Petronelle the best portion of her dowry."

"Like our father did for you."

George immediately regretted his comment as the ladies fell silent and plied their needles more diligently now. Petronelle flipped the pages in her book absently, the slap of parchment against parchment irritating. Elinor sent the children out and made an exasperated sound, glaring at him. "One day, my lord, that tongue of yours will be the undoing of your family," she hissed.

"I was only stating a fact. My father took the lady Maud for her beauty and grace, her piety, which are still the envy of Cumbria," George remarked, shrugging, and turned to pick up the Bible and set it back on the prie-dieu. He noticed Joanna watching and smiled at her.

"No need for flattery, George," Maud sighed and she turned away from the ladies and her son. He could have sworn there were tears in her eyes.

"Goose!" Petronelle whispered. "We don't talk of Father or even mention his name!" She nodded towards Joanna. "That pretty little bird you brought from Grasmere watches you, Brother. I imagine her dower price could be bargained for, or should I have said bower?"

George glanced over just when Joanna's eyes fell back to her needlework. "Choose your words carefully, Petra!" he whispered none-too-sweetly. He rose and went to stand behind Joanna, watching silently as the needle flashed in the sunlight and brought colored silks in and out of the coarsely woven linen until what looked to be the outline of a bird appeared.

George gestured at the frame of cloth in the girl's lap. "Your work is exceptional, Joanna; perhaps when you have time you'd make a scarf for my helmet? I'd wear it to the lists."

"My lord earl is strangely interested in women's work."

"Only to find out what a lady does when the men are away," George replied.

"Sir, you will be sadly mistaken to learn that you're not as interesting as you think you are—and we don't talk about you except to tally up your sins," Elinor spoke up.

"If you continue, Elinor, I'll have a very different picture painted of you than the one I've kept in my heart for so long," George quipped.

"I've heard it said that absence never made the heart grow fonder where it concerned the earls of Grasmere," came the tart reply.

"I could have died on the battlefield screaming your name and it still would not have been good enough for you, Mistress Longleate."

"But you lived, and that's the sadder part!"

"Enough!" Maud snapped. "What's done is done! Elinor, you shame yourself with this childish display —you married the greatest lord in Cumbria next to my son! And George, do us all a favor and find something worthwhile to take up your time now that you're home—or find a wife!"

"Or another mistress . . ." Elinor curtsied and retreated to a corner with a book, watching George and Joanna with narrowed suspicious eyes.

"I shall light a candle for you, brother," Petronelle whispered.

"Why?" he asked, pulling on her braid.

"Ow! Stop that! You would have been safer staying in the Holy Land!" his sister giggled. George failed to recognize the jest and sat down at a small table where a chess game was set, moving the heavy ivory and onyx pieces around in a battle formation.

"We could use a good man to survey our lands and go with William to collect the rents," Maud said.

"Not acquainted with any."

"Pardon?" Maud looked up, brows raised.

"Good men, that is. I'm not acquainted with any."

"I know it will take some time to get used to being the lord of Grasmere; now is the best time to start."

"I'm no sooner returned than you want me gone again," George murmured, moving a pawn.

"There is more damage to Grasmere that needs mending than just the stones and timber," Maud answered. She glanced sideways at him and saw his frown, knew it had the effect she wanted, for George squirmed and pushed the board away.

"You were in check," Joanna said, not bothering

to look up from her needlework.

"Why don't you find a stag to kill or do something else that entertains men?" Petronelle suggested.

"I think I'll go for a ride," said George after he glanced at Joanna, and offering a chivalric bow, swept out of the solar.

"Wait!"

George was halfway to the stable yard when he heard Joanna's shout. She was sprinting over the muddy ground, the hems of her expensive skirts glazed by snow. "They're all geese!" Joanna said breathlessly to an unasked question when she caught up with him.

"The women?"

"Every last one of them, my lord. Please do not make me stay in their company. I would die of boredom, or I would kill them, and then the priest and the sheriff would have reason to burn me - or hang me. Please?"

"That is not my decision to make; the countess will have a say about that, Joanna."

"I did not ask to be brought here."

"You may leave at any time."

"I've given that some thought." Joanna said, stepping forward, arms crossed defiantly in the manner George hated – the stance that meant a confrontation.

"You know the way back to the village, I suppose?" George queried, pointing the way past the gates. "Consider the benefits, however, of being in the earl of Grasmere's hall compared to the bowers and kitchens of Butcher Lane." He studied her for a moment, and then started toward the stables again. "Pretty dress," he said over his shoulder.

"For this I give thanks to Lady Petronelle, for it was she who took clothes from her own coffers since I have none of my own," Joanna said as she hurried to catch him up. "I might befriend her for this kindness."

George chuckled. "She is a lady with a grand opinion of herself and her accomplishments, though they be few and far between. Are you certain you would have her for a friend, or that she would want you?"

"I do not see why not, my Lord. We are not very different."

Now George stopped and he turned, trying to suppress a laugh. "Do you think so, Mistress Fletcher? Perhaps it is that high opinion of yourself that makes you so much like her?"

"I speak truly, sir!" Joanna snapped. She caressed the glossy fur cuff of bell-shaped sleeve of her gown and then held it out, saying "I used to have many dresses like this!"

"Used?"

"Before. When my father wasn't in disgrace, before the King's men came…" Joanna stopped, and glanced over to see the look of surprise George gave her. "You thought I was a jade, didn't you? In most men's eyes, women are either saints or whores."

George gave her a sideways grin and reached for her hand, guiding her so that she could avoid a puddle.

"And here I thought you were a nobleman, not a gentleman," Joanna remarked.

"I'm lots of things, but let's save our places in life for another day," George quipped. "You ought to get back to your needlework before they find you missing."

"The ladies treat me as if I was a boil, or a plague. You're the only one who talks to me—even if the words and meaning are sharp."

"My mother the countess takes some getting used to, and Elinor—well, there's no explanation or apology for her."

"Sometimes all a woman wants is to hear an apology," Joanna said matter-of-factly. "To hear the words 'I'm sorry' will do a world of good and costs less than a trinket."

"Return to the bower, Joanna," George sighed and turned her gently towards the donjon before he disappeared into the stables. He was brushing down Aubrey's favorite white Arabian when he noticed that the light had changed. Looking up, he saw the silhouette of the girl in the entrance of the stable.

"You're like a stray puppy." he quipped. "I can look no further than over my shoulder and find you there."

"I've never seen a horse as fine as this!" Joanna murmured, venturing forward. "Is he yours?"

"Now he is—used to be my father's."

"May God assoil him."

"He's not dead—he's a contemplative now."

"A monk? Your father would forsake his wife and family, give up this castle, to pray all day?"

"Well, some think prayer does us a world of good." George said. He continued to brush down the stallion's flanks and glanced at Joanna out of the corner of his eyes. "Aren't you worried about your virtue, Mistress? Of being compromised by being in my company? The lady Elinor painted a nasty portrait of me, and a gentlewoman would take care."

"I know the difference between truth and jealousy. It's no concern of mine what people think," Joanna said. "They ought to be at their prayers."

George laughed at this and handed Joanna the brush so that she could take a turn. They spent a pleasant hour at this, talking of horses, childhoods dissimilar but similar in some ways until they heard a clarion and the rumble of a mounted host.

"My lord!"

William Longleate's shout brought George to the stable entrance. Looking out, he watched the approach of a noble retinue, the banners and men unfamiliar. It was a small party, no more than twenty, but George knew even six well-armed knights could do much evil. He took a sword from one of the household knights and shouted at him to raise the garrison.

CHAPTER 4

J OANNA, COME BACK with me; it's safer than staying here," George ordered when she started to retreat into the stable.

Joanna shook her head violently and stepped further into one of the stalls, grabbing a post to stand her ground as George and one of the knights approached.

"God's life! They've found me at last!" she whispered; her cry muffled by the shouts of men heading for the donjon. "No, I dare not! Let me stay here, sir! Please! Oh Sweet Gesu, they've found me!"

George pried Joanna's hands from the post and led her out, the household knights surrounding them in a shield wall as they ran towards the donjon. "No one will harm you, Joanna. Did I not promise you yester eve? Stay close now."

Expecting the alarms to sound, George was puzzled by the lack of activity in the household. Had Skelwith been without a lord so long that it forgot how to muster for battle? He stopped short when William Longleate stepped in his path and bowed low, waving at the party now drawing up before the donjon steps.

"A delegation from Arkengarthdale, my lord," William said.

It was a friendly contingent for as George

approached three of their number fell back
respectfully, smiling, and bowed in greeting. As they
stepped away, the old man from Deadman's Last
hobbled forward. He leaned painfully on his staff and
struggled for every breath. Likewise, George felt as if
he had been punched in the chest. The air seemed to
have been sucked out of him. Bits and pieces of
childhood now flooded his memory and this old man
was in every vignette his mind conjured—vile,
unhappy memories, at that.

"I know this man!" George whispered and his
words were tinged with fear.

"He asked for your lord father," William replied.
"I of course explained to him the circumstance, but
he would not leave until speaking with you."

"Not until I've spoken with the countess!"

"He apparently knows your family and swears to
have been a vassal of Ascalon at one time," William
continued as they hurried along. George absently
nodded.

Why didn't I recognize him? I should have
known who he was last night! George thought. The
old man had haunted his childhood and always
seemed to be where George was, even when riding in
Kentmere Forest or swimming in Grasmere.
Whenever George was alone, the old man appeared
and watched him, an evil smile stretched across his
lips. So many years later, he had returned, and yet
looked the same. Now George was visited by a
familiar sick feeling, the hot and cold of sweat that
came with fear. He picked up speed and suddenly was
compelled to run to the Great hall where he was
certain his mother would be. Maud was nowhere to

be found. He spun about and made for the solar
staircase. Williams and several servants scrambled to
follow. Only Joanna hesitated.

"I should have no part in this council," Joanna
balked, as she fell back and curtsied. Before George
could protest, she added, "I'll go to the chapel. I'll be
safe there." Joanna went down, the hems of her skirts
whispering on the stone, servants and retainers
making a path for her and bowing respectfully as if
she was a great lady.

Richildis of Eskeleth and her man Stephen turned
from a conversation with Maud and Petronelle when
George entered the solar unannounced with his party,
swords drawn, shields held close. Stephen swept the
floor with a bow while Richildis merely nodded in
acknowledgment. With a shake of his head, George
dismissed his men. He came forward with sword in
hand, nevertheless, keeping his eyes on Richildis.

"Here you are! Lady, here is the count of
Grasmere, my son George Ascalon," Maud said, and
beckoned him to take the cup of mead offered. Her
movements were static and seemed born of anxiety,
and for once she looked at George squarely, as if to
plead. George accepted the cup and took a drink,
mindful that his hand shook, and that all eyes were on
him. He studied Richildis over the rim of his chalice,
the image of his father's icon dancing in his mind's
eye.

"Lady, good day. Why did you never say a word
yester evening? That you had business with Grasmere,
I mean," George demanded in a cool, impersonal
tone.

"Do you mean to say you already know the Lady

of Eskeleth?" Maud asked, her eyes darting from George to Richildis and back again in a way he recognized—the way his mother looked at a girl she disapproved of, or thought her son had bedded.

"Our meeting was brief—at Deadman's Last. Had she told me she was coming to Skelwith, I would have escorted her party. As it was—"

"As it was, Lady Countess, we were distracted from our business with Grasmere," Stephen interrupted. "My lady's maid was ill and her devotion to this girl was such that she could not leave her side."

"True Christian charity!" Maud sighed happily.

"Commendable," George remarked.

"We saw how you were attentive to the girl—your concern was commendable," Stephen simpered. "Our men said that you spoke with them and touched the girl without fear. She was greatly recovered soon after-wards and they swear you have a gift for healing!"

"Truly?" Maud asked, looking at George in a new light, a smile crossing her lips.

"All worked out for the best," Stephen continued, "and we spent our evening in prayer to prepare ourselves for this meeting."

"For what? What have you heard about me?" George laughed into the chalice. He thumped it on a table and wiped his mouth with his sleeve, turning to look at Richildis, and it was a careful study of her; the physical interest of last night replaced by trepidation. "Perhaps your lady will explain how well she is acquainted with my father?" he asked.

Richildis glanced up sharply, frowning. "I'm sure

you are mistaken in that, sir. I do not know your father."

"I assure you I am not. My father carries your likeness."

"How can that be? I have never seen your father."

"George," Maud warned.

"Perhaps you inspired a painter to make a likeness for him? Were you lovers at one time?"

Richildis looked him straight in the eyes. "I do not know your father, lord Grasmere, and it would be a grave insult to your lady mother if true. I am nothing but common."

"I am too sure as to be contrary!"

"George, Richildis is here to redeem a pledge. I fear this is something we should have spoken of years ago; you are called to champion—" Maud interrupted but he waved her off.

"The old man at Deadman's Last! Why did you not acknowledge him as one of your retainers?" George demanded of Richildis.

"Should I acknowledge every farmer, baker, and milkmaid on my father's lands for your pleasure?" she asked coolly.

"I know him—he used to spy on the castle when I was boy!"

"George! Save your interrogation for another day, or perhaps on the way to Eskeleth," Maud laughed uneasily.

"I have no desire to go into Arkengarthdale," he sniped.

"You have no choice. A pledge was made to the lady's father."

"Let the lady's father and mine settle their

account." George answered. "I'm looking for a quiet life now."

"My lord commands you," Stephen said. He came forward and handed George an ancient scroll. "Here is the accord between our houses. Read it, and you'll see that Eskeleth and Grasmere have an agreement—to assist one another in time of need, such as now. There is a dangerous enemy that has taken hold of Arkengarthdale; in particular, my lord Wulfstan's seat of Eskeleth."

George made a cursory review of the accord and handed it back. "This enterprise is too costly for me; I have no provisions to spare," he apologized sincerely. "I've only just returned from the Levant without men or arms. I cannot agree to help anyone. And as I've said, I have no heart for war. The lady is welcome to stay on Grasmere lands with her father and household if she is threatened."

"I pray you, sir," Richildis interrupted, coming forward with long, elegant hands outstretched, "I beg you to reconsider. If Grasmere was threatened and its people taken into slavery and forced to submit to great evil, my father would honor the accord he made with yours."

George studied her exquisitely beautiful face and saw something there he had not seen before—a coldness, a reserve that would not easily be breached, even with the most gentle of words or lovemaking. But there was also vulnerability for he noticed that she was trembling much as Joanna had in the stable and in a moment of compassion, he reached for Richildis' hand, but she pulled away.

"Sir, I do pray you."

"Madam, I tell you again, I cannot do this. Not now," George answered softly. "You would not send a man on his deathbed to plow a field or ride to the hunt. Why then must you ask a man sick of war to take up his sword?"

"You know in your heart you must do this!" Richildis cried.

"You know nothing of me, Madam," said George icily.

"Your father made a promise to mine! Your father swore Wulfstan of Eskeleth was a man of honor equal to his. I think not! There is no honor in Grasmere. Your father left us to fight alone and we suffered greatly!"

"Your father sent a hundred men to fight with the French and Venetians in the Holy Land—"

"So he did."

"How many of those men have returned to their homes and families, Lady?"

"I know not, sir. But they went willingly to Jerusalem to take it from the infidels!"

"No, they did not," George replied. "That is, they did not go to Jerusalem."

"Where did they go then, if you're so knowledgeable?"

"To Constantinople."

"That is a lie."

"And who are you to say? Were you there, Lady, when men sworn to defend Christendom and take the Holy Land from the infidels went instead to Byzantium? Did you hear the blind fool, Dandolo, the doge of Venice, cajole and plead with good men to destroy Constantinople so that he might control all the trade routes to the east? Were you there, Madam, when that city was pillaged in the name of Christ? Were you there when women and children were slaughtered and the precious relics of our Holy Mother Church were plundered and given to soldiers and knights as wages?"

"I only meant to say—"

"I mean to say that good knights of England swore to take the Holy Land back from the infidels and found themselves alongside Venetians in the plunder and rape of Constantinople! The city of our Christian brothers! Your father had no qualms about it and put to death those who would question him!"

"You are unkind, sir. No better man lives," she replied quietly.

"The timbre of your voice would say otherwise."

Richildis glanced up and George drew a breath when he saw how livid and bright her large eyes had become. Something else was there, however, and it was something he didn't like, and couldn't name.

"My father is beset with worries no man could possibly understand or have suffered!" she said.

"When he has wasted thirty-six months in the service of a lord who cares nothing for what his soldiers believe or feel; when he has spent weeks on end watching the slaughter of innocent people in the name of a man who preached love; when he has held his dying friends in his arms, then I would believe you!" George replied angrily. He turned to his mother. "Madam, I am not a soldier for hire!"

"George, at least hear them!" Maud pleaded.

"I have come home to care for my family and my estates. I'm done with war."

"My lord Grasmere, what if the enemy was beyond all reason?" Stephen proffered.

"Do you mean Dandolo or the Pope?"

"George!" Maud cried, exasperated.

"The enemy we speak of is no less evil than that which you fought in Constantinople and brought you to this unhappy state," Richildis spoke up.

"You do not know me well enough, Madam, to pass such judgment!" George answered curtly, liking her less and less. "I've made my decision. If you desire shelter or protection here on my lands and in my house, you shall have it. That is all I can afford."

George fled, taking the stairs of Ravenglass Tower by twos, servants scattering as he stormed past them. He didn't stop until he was in his own chambers and went out onto the balcony that looked out over the lakes and mountains of Cumbria, standing there and letting the sun warm his sweating face.

He was trembling. His hands began to shake violently and George clenched them as he done so many times before on the voyages from Byzantium and the Holy Land, as he had in the inns and monasteries that boarded him on the long journey back to England, as he had during the many nights when he woke from unspeakable horrors that crowded his mind no matter how hard he tried to forget. George pounded them against the stone parapet until the skin was broken and the sandstone was tinted a dark rose with his blood, until the spasm ended. When the muscles finally relaxed, he slumped down and wept and remained there until the shadows lengthened and the vespers bell rang.

A succession of light raps on the door warned George to make himself presentable and to show himself a man, for Petronelle was outside. She made an exasperated sound when George opened the door a bit and let it swing wider to let her in.

"I told them to leave you be. I know what it's like to hold the memories too close," Petronelle said when the door closed again. "Lucy's wounds! George, what have you done to your hands?"

"It's nothing."

"Nothing! You didn't put your fists through a glass pane again? Oh, you poor fool!"

"I don't need your pity!"

"And you'll get none from me."

"Go away, damn you!"

"No. I've come to say I agree with you. You were right to turn them away. We haven't the men to defend a cow byre."

"I suppose in between times spent seducing the local nobility you studied the household accounts?" George asked as he washed his wounds and bandaged them. "It's not your concern, Petra; you're not the earl of Grasmere."

"Oh, don't play the great lord with me! You couldn't care a fig about honoring this accord of Father's. You're more disappointed that Richildis is a cold, cruel bitch and for the first time your easy charm and seduction failed."

"It wasn't the first time,"

"What?"

"Never mind."

"I do believe that's the true reason you won't help her; not that you haven't the men or arms."

"I told you . . ."

Petronelle chose an apple from the bowl on the window sill and tossed it at George, who caught it.

"Then perhaps you should accept the commission. If you're not so eager to have your bed go cold with this ice maiden, it will be all the easier. And once a thing is done, it's done. You may come home and do whatever it was you came home to do."

"I can't do it."

"Others will call you a coward."

"Let them!"

"You've been in the heat of battle. How bad could this be?"

George picked up his sword and balanced it, then offered it to Petronelle. "Take it, sister. No, don't shirk. Come then."

"You want me to prove myself?" Petronelle laughed and grabbed the sword when George tossed it. She cursed as the weight of it made her stagger back.

"Could you kill a man holding that—or struggle to hold it and use it when your strength is sapped and the enemy is all around and there's no chance of escape?"

"I take your meaning,"

"Would you?"

"Enough, George!"

"Answer me!"

"Yes, I could and I would!" Petronelle hissed, coming at him. "I would fight for every last man, woman, and child—and the last donkey in a stable— if it were my home and mine to protect! If I were called to this duty I would do it. Will you, brother?"

"Petra," George began and then tossed the apple back.

"Will you?" She touched his cheek with a soft, warm hand and then kissed it. "Make it your one last act of chivalry and do this for your poor sister—a wedding present."

"Italian silks or French linens wouldn't be enough?"

"You know me better." Petronelle answered. "So?"

"So, you've won again—and I hate it when you win," George said with a sad smile.

"Come then; Mother will be pleased to hear you've changed your mind," Petronelle said as she went for the door.

"I'll be along shortly."

George waited until the echo of her footsteps faded and then hurried out of the donjon and went straight to the chapel.

Joanna wasn't there. He went out and glanced around, noticing soldiers and servants going about their respective businesses, but no Joanna. George turned to go back into the donjon when he saw her standing on a bench at the dovecote, feeding the birds.

"The cats will be grateful to you—you're fattening up their quarry," he greeted.

Joanna looked down, surprised to find George. She put the dove on her hand into the cote and closed the screen gently, so as not to startle the birds.

"I've come to tell you that I must go away," George sighed. He couldn't help but notice how surprised she looked at this.

"Why tell me this, sir? I am only a woman of the household, as you have made it plain."

"I shouldn't have brought you here to live without knowing what to expect. You made it plain that you have no care for the women here and without me to protect you, well, you are free to go."

She frowned and after studying his face a moment, said, "Thank you, my lord. You've made it easier than I could hope for. I didn't want to escape in the dead of night from the bower. Thank you once again for your chivalry, though it is misplaced. I can take care of myself."

"You'll stay?"

"No; I only wonder about your interest in what I should think of this news, which doesn't seem to please you."

"It doesn't—I am held to an oath; something of my father's—it's a matter of some importance, I'm told. So there it is. Good day to you, Mistress."

As he turned to leave Joanna said, "Perhaps we will meet in London," she said matter-of-factly.

He turned back. "London? Why would you go there?"

"To find my father."

"Alone?"

Joanna stepped down from the bench and in doing so George caught the fragrance of cut flowers and something else—citrus and frankincense. The mingling of scents was intoxicating. "Alone is how you found me, my lord," she said with a smile. "If you give me the loan of a horse and a servant, I could be gone in the morning. And if I find my father, he will see that your horse and servant are returned and in good care and coin for your trouble."

"London is a great place; where do you expect to find him?"

"In William de Braose's house or at court, if I arrive by Christmas. And so farewell."

George followed her, having no trouble keeping up with Joanna's quick steps. "De Braose? He must have some influence."

"At one time he did. As much as any Welshman could have in England if only to survive and have possession of one's lands in Wales." Joanna laughed and shook her head so that the scent of citrus, frankincense, and wildflowers bewitched him again. "Ah, there's that look again! You think I tell stories."

"What if I escorted you to London—after I returned from my business in the Yorkshire dales?"

"You have more important business at hand; escorting a lady to London is better left in the care of one of your most trusted, good, and decent men."

"Then it should be me," George answered.

"You trust no one else? I fear I shall be greater in debt to you for these kindnesses you continue to show. I do not belong here. It's better I should find my father and make a new life."

"If you think so. Goodbye, then, Mistress Fletcher." He said quietly and extended his hand. Joanna saw the stained bandages and looked at him curiously. Rather than accept his courtesy, Joanna nodded and hurried away.

✠✠✠

GEORGE FOUND A somber tableau waiting in the solar. He received a kiss from Petronelle, who retreated to her usual footstool in a corner and nodded in the direction of the others. Maud was reading her omnipresent Bible while William and Stephen studied a map and spoke quietly, almost in whispers, so as not to disturb her mediation. Richildis was seated in a window seat, staring at nothing in particular. George made for the window seat but stopped when he saw the hard set of Richildis' eyes and the tightly pursed mouth. She seemed to change by the minute, George thought, and not pleasantly. Her eyes moved up and down, making an assessment, and narrowed when she asked, "What have you done to your hands?"

"My falcons weren't that excited to welcome me home," he lied, glancing at Petronelle. He approached Stephen. "I've come to tell you I've changed my mind," he announced.

Stephen glanced up sharply, exclaiming, "This is glad news indeed! I'll have my clerk send word to Lord Wulfstan—his household guard will meet us at the frontier and escort us to Arkengarthdale."

"When shall we leave?" Richildis spoke up; keeping her eyes on whatever had fascinated her outside in the bailey.

"The roads over the fells will be impossible until the spring thaw; that is our chief consideration, and I must summon my vassals."

"If it is possible for our small party to travel over these same fells and roads to Cumbria, I see no reason why you cannot lead us home!" Richildis snapped.

"Why should you call for vassals?" Stephen interrupted. "All that is required is a handful of men."

"Even a handful of men require provisions,

horses, and armor. We have no ancient magic to provide for us as Arthur had on his quest for the Holy Grail, nor do we have archangels to guide our way," George quipped, but his humor was lost.

"Waiting until the spring will only make matters worse for us!"

"Lady, if you require my assistance, then you will accept my terms," George said coldly and quietly. "We leave as soon as spring comes. Will you return with us or wait here?"

Richildis turned slowly and stared at George as if seeing him for the first time, and then frowned. "I'll come with you. But I will need an escort, for you will remember that my handmaiden lies at the inn in Grasmere and the journey back would surely kill her. A daughter of a good family, her father a knight, perhaps, would content me. We'll take no finery, and wear soldiers' clothes, if you like. We will carry weapons—and use them if we must."

"Will you now?" George scoffed.

"She needn't look further," said Petronelle brightly. "I would be glad to accompany my brother."

"I forbid it!" Maud snapped. "Petronelle, you are to be married in three weeks' time. Lady Richildis, any of the daughters of the mayor of Grasmere would be worthy companions—he has eight, all educated in the convent."

"I said, a good family," Richildis purred.

"I'd wager a sovereign that the lord mayor's girls are quiet and demure; they'd steal no light from you," George sniped back.

"Better still, brother, have little Joanna accompany her ladyship. For all we know, she's a cast-off princess; how else to explain the way she carries herself?" Petronelle giggled and was suddenly quiet when she saw that her brother failed to recognize the humor or the impolite dig at Richildis made for his amusement.

"Mistress Fletcher has it in mind to go to London to seek her father. But if she were coming with us, I would think her a suitable companion."

"I meant that in jest! Surely you see that I am the only lady fit for the task!" Petronelle cried.

"I doubt if Chester would wait to claim his bride while you play at warrior, Petra."

"Why is it that everything I do is inconsequential, George?" growled his sister.

Maud closed the Bible noisily and glared at her children. "Petronelle, need I remind you of your duty? George, stop tormenting your sister. You have much to do before the journey north."

"Perhaps learn how to be a nobleman," Richildis sniffed.

"If the lady finds our company so disgusting, she may go elsewhere," George responded quietly.

"Indeed I would, if an invitation were made."

William cleared his throat and stepped forward. "We have apartments for your ladyship," he said. "My lord Stephen, if you would join us? Allow me to show you the way."

"Hopefully to hell, or straight off a cliff!" Petronelle muttered as they left.

"Petronelle!" Maud said sharply. "I would expect as much from your brother!"

"Pardon, Madam," said Petronelle and melted into a deep curtsy. She looked up at her mother and smiled. "And you should expect the same courage and boldness from me. I can think of no better companion for George than myself on this quest."

"It is out of the question," Maud now stated flatly.

"It's such a small thing I ask! Gentlemen are asked to prove themselves before they wed—why not a maiden?"

"A point well taken, Petra," George commented. "If a lady had the strength to defend herself with a sword or ax, she would be formidable—if she could survive the assault."

"A woman in danger is no less courageous than a man. Give me half a chance and I'll prove you wrong!"

"You are to be married in three weeks' time!" he argued.

"You play favorites, George! If Mistress Fletcher were fat and ugly, would you be so eager to let her come along? Bonny though she is, she looks frail enough—if she picked up a sword she would break in two—"

"I will hear no more!" Maud cried. "We will speak of this no more today, nor tomorrow."

Maud swept out of the solar, slamming the door behind her.

"The matter is not concluded as far as I'm concerned," Petronelle spoke up. "And we *will* speak of it tomorrow!"

CHAPTER 5

T HE MATTER WAS the topic of conversation at supper that evening. The magistrates of Little Langdale had been invited to dine and they could talk of nothing else save this new heroic quest assigned to the young earl. Stories and memories of misspent youth and dreams of crusade and glory were shared and passed on, growing more bold, impossible, and mythical as the wine flowed. George managed to stay out of the conversations and merely smiled and raised a cup when asked about his own exploits, avoiding the subject altogether. He was more interested in one lady sitting at a lower table with the rest of the women of the household, one who had arrived late to the feast.

He'd been engrossed in a conversation about exporting wool to Italy with a merchant from Little Langdale when he noticed that a girl had entered alone and gone unnoticed by most of the guests, but not for long. When his companions began to remark on the girl's beauty and make crude wagers on how biddable she might be, George silenced them, stating quietly that his friend Mistress Fletcher would not be used for their sport.

As soon as the musicians struck a tune, he rose, and all eyes watched, expecting him to invite the lady Richildis to dance. Instead, he offered his hand to

Joanna. Two gentlemen bowed away, deferring their hopeful places to George.

"Should you not have chosen your sister or lady Richildis to partner?" Joanna asked as they stepped off.

"Should you not be on your way to London?" he countered. "Or couldn't you find a good and decent man to escort you?"

"Good and decent men are far from lacking, my lord; I have unfinished business here before I go."

"What business is that?"

"To repay a debt."

"I know you haven't any money."

"In right action, my lord. Lady Petronelle sent word to me that the gentlewoman from Eskeleth requires a lady to accompany her on your journey to Arkengarthdale. I offer my service to her, and to Grasmere—if consent is given."

"It is granted. But there is a problem; the lady requires a woman from a good family."

"My father is as good as any English lord; she will have to take me as I am—a good daughter to a good man."

"I'll take your word on that, Mistress."

"There is one more consideration," Joanna added. "You must allow the lady Petronelle to come with you."

"Ah, she's gotten to you, has she?" George laughed.

"No; I see the necessity. Give her what she wants now and you'll reap the reward for your generosity."

At that moment in the dance they met with Petronelle and her escort, a lawyer from Grasmere, and changed partners for the next measures.

"Not home twenty-four hours, Brother, and you are the subject of gossip again," Petronelle murmured to George. "She's pretty, clever, and surprising, that Joanna."

"You thought enough of her to suggest she attend Richildis."

"Because I know you have a good opinion of her, and what pleases you, pleases me."

"That hasn't always been the case, has it? You may persuade Mother as you always do, but don't think for one moment I've changed my mind."

Petronelle smiled sweetly at the lawyer when he came back to partner her, and then shot George with a none-too loving glare before she danced away, saying over her shoulder, "I will have the last word in the matter, George!"

Taking Joanna's hand again, George nodded, and then saw both Elinor and Richildis staring daggers at him.

Going into battle again would be preferable to hearing another word from Petronelle, standing toe to toe with the women staring him down, or trying to understand women at all, especially the girl from Butcher's Lane who was proving to be someone no one expected her to be.

What that was, George thought as he smiled and glided past Joanna, he had yet to figure out and was almost afraid of the conclusion.

CHAPTER 6

ETRONELLE KEPT HER word and dominated conversations at breakfast, in the chapel, and on trips to the market in Little Langdale or Grasmere; every syllable, every phrase, extolling her virtues and strengths, her pedigree and her beauty, and why she should accompany George on the adventure looming before him.

"You give me no alternative, Petra. We'll have no choice but to unleash you on Wulfstan's enemy," George muttered as they arrived in Grasmere market on a clear winter morning.

"Do you mean I shall go with you?" Petronelle asked hopefully.

"What I believe he means, my lady, is that the enemy would probably kill themselves rather than listen to you go on and on about your splendid attributes—I know I'm of like mind!" Elinor quipped.

"The lake is that way, Elinor. Don't let us detain you a moment longer!"

"Petronelle, your future has been decided and we cannot afford to insult a man as powerful as Chester," George interjected, hoping to stave a fight.

Petronelle made an exasperated sound and smiled at a young knight who passed by. "Chester is not the only wealthy lord in England, brother. I suppose you might find another at court if he cannot abide my independence!"

"Ah . . . sheep!" exclaimed George as they rounded a corner and saw the pens of gray faced Dartmoors brought from the pastures at Skelwith.

And so the argument continued as George proudly watched his sheep fetch a pretty price, as they wound through the market in search of delicacies and gifts for their Christmas celebration and as George greeted old friends. He pretended to listen, nodded in agreement and smiled on cue for his sister's benefit.

They had reached the blacksmith's when George suddenly stopped, distracted, paying no attention to Petronelle as she walked on. He stood paralyzed, mindless of the people jostling and trying to get past him in the market square.

"Lord, not again!" Elinor spat and began searching in her scrip for something.

"What is it?" Joanna asked, joining her.

"He used to have fits when a boy and I'm sure one has come upon him. We all carry a restorative."

Elinor's words fell on absent ears, for Joanna had left her side and gently passed through a wave of marketgoers to where George stood. She had no cause to ask what had brought him to a standstill. The ubiquitous old man in the blue gown, the man that seemed to scare George, was standing in the doorway of a shop. Despite the man's benign appearance Joanna felt afraid and without thinking touched George's arm.

"Pardon my lord; we should go with the others."

"Stay back!" George hissed.

"I don't understand . . ."

"Move—before it's too late!" he growled, shoving

her off, and grabbed a weapon that lay against the door of the blacksmith's, running towards the old man.

"George!" Petronelle screamed.

He heard nothing and saw nothing but a whirlwind of mist that covered the market square and when it dissolved unveiled a hideous creature. This was not the scaled beast with glowing eyes that haunted his dreams since childhood, but a dark being, a knight putrid and decaying, the skin and muscle sagging on bones writhing with worms and oozing pustules, the face half gnawed away. George closed his eyes and attacked. He heard the beast's screams, and inhaled a stench that made him want to vomit. He swung again and fell, waiting for death—and then opened his eyes.

He was lying on the ground in the market, the sword in his hand. The old man was gone. The air was filled with the good scent of wet earth and produce, of livestock and spices, things that meant home and life. Joanna and Petronelle were standing over him, while Elinor stood apart with the servants, watching from a safe distance.

"Oh, my poor brother!" Petronelle sobbed. "Someone help him!"

Joanna bent down and picked up the sword and gave it to the bewildered blacksmith with whispered thanks. She waited for George to catch his breath. "Shall I help you up, sir?" she asked.

He nodded and stood with some difficulty, noticing the stares of the marketgoers and, in particular, Elinor. "You go on," George said to Petronelle as he drew ragged breaths. "We'll follow."

Joanna noticed that she still held George's hand and arm and quickly released him; she was surprised when he took her hand again.

"What did you see?" George asked quietly, his breath coming evenly now, the color returning to his face.

She shook her head, gazed down at the patch of mud and snow that left an imprint where George had fallen and shook her head.

"Tell me the truth, Joanna. Please."

"Something," she whispered, choking back tears. "I felt afraid. I don't know what it was—I was afraid. It was—something."

"But you did see it?"

"George?" Petronelle called.

Ignoring stares and whispers, George strode with difficulty out of the market square to join his sister and their companions, and was relieved when Petronelle took up her litany of qualities on the way home. Every now and then he glanced at Joanna, who kept her eyes straight ahead and nodded or smiled absently whenever someone spoke.

Empty gestures that spoke volumes.

That evening, he found Joanna alone in the chapel. He slipped in quietly and saw that she was deep in prayer, the colored stones of her prayer beads catching sparks of light from the candles as they slid through her fingers one at a time.

When Joanna completed her devotion she sighed, and George could see how her shoulders relaxed.

"What do you pray for?" he said aloud.

As expected, his salutation made her start and even in the dim light of the chapel, he recognized that fearful look.

"That God should grant me a peaceful night, and keep me safe," she answered self-consciously as she tucked away the beads.

"From the likes of madmen like me?"

"I think, my lord, that if I had cause to fear you, it would have been when you took me from Butcher's Lane," Joanna said brightly as she gathered her things to leave. As she passed, she dipped in a fluid bow at the waist. George took her hand.

"What did you see today?" he whispered.

"Sir, I beg of you," Joanna began. When she saw his intent, earnest face, she took the beads from her scrip and held them out. George took them after a moment while he studied her pretty face, took particular interest in how the color of her eyes changed, and how her steady gaze had softened.

"Joanna, I saw how frightened you were—you would not have looked so if, like the others, you'd seen nothing."

She looked away, and George could see the gleam of tears in her eyes.

"I saw death."

CHAPTER 7

T HE NOISE WAS a strangely familiar and unsettling sound, coming in and out of George's dream until it was so loud he woke with a start.

It was no dream!

Hugh, his servant, had crawled off his pallet at the same time and grumbled about going to see if they were under siege, for the sound was unmistakable: the shouting of men, barking of hounds, horses galloping and the ringing of metal on metal. George flew out of bed and dressed. His heart pounded and he felt sick.

Not today, he prayed as he ran through the family living quarters, struggling to fasten a brigandine over his shirt. Not today of all days!

"Hugh! My sword! And quickly!" George hissed, shoving the man back in the direction they came. Scrambling down the staircase into the great hall, George had his answer.

The dogs were yelping happily and circling Maud, who was supervising decorations for Petronelle's wedding feast and guests were arriving with retinues in tow. He sucked in a huge breath and expelled it quickly in relief, retracing his path to Ravenglass Tower and ignoring the bewildered stares and amused grins of household retainers and servants as he went.

Hugh met him in the tower stairwell and handed

over the sword. "I suppose we're not under siege, my lord?"

"Only by my sister's bridegroom and friends," George muttered, going past him into the bedchamber. "Find me something to drink."

A blast of trumpets announced the arrival of more wedding guests.

"Christ Jesus and all his bloody saints!" Hugh swore when the clarion startled him and he spilled wine on George. "Forgive me, Sir! I suppose we'll have to listen to that all day."

"At least it isn't the Venetian army on our backs. Here, let me," George said and took the towel from Hugh and sopped up the richly-colored wine. For a moment George thought he was bandaging a horrific wound on his own arm, sinew and bone exposed in a great gaping slash that ran the length of his forearm from wrist to elbow. He shuddered and threw down the towel. "Something to eat!" George hissed to the question of where he was going. He went back down to the great hall.

"Good morning, George," Maud greeted. Her brows arched in amusement at the sight of the brigandine and mail shirt. "I had hoped you would wear something more formal for your sister's wedding. You're giving the bride away."

"It looks like an army assembling out in the bailey. Who are all these men?"

"Need you ask? The earl of Chester's household and wedding guests," said Petronelle cheerfully. "It does look as if he brought an entire garrison with him; no doubt he needs to prove that he is more powerful than my brother of Grasmere. He never did like you, George."

Petronelle was standing on a bench while her serving women stitched her into a magnificent wedding dress of gold embroidered silk, lacing the seams tight about every curve so that it wouldn't have mattered if she was naked before the world—her charm was very apparent.

"The only threat to Chester is a change of heart," said George over his shoulder.

"Yes, I know." Petronelle hopped down from the bench and scuffed across the room to join George at the window. Her women squealed in protest as she took the hems through dirty rushes and the leavings of last night's banquet, meat bones to spilled wine. "And I know that's why he brought all these men—to keep me to my promise. How very like a French virelai, or chanson all this is; unfortunately, I don't have a mysterious knight to arrive just as the bishop asks if there is anyone who knows of an impediment to the marriage."

"Is there?"

"Of course not! But it would be nice if someone came and championed me, took me to some far off castle to make love to me."

"Dear, oh dear . . . !"

"I wish I could run away. I'd go to your hiding place."

George turned sharply and frowned. "How did you know—?"

"I've known about it for years—I used to follow you when you rode off after fighting with Mother and Father about whatever it was that tormented your soul that day. Besides, it's not much of a hiding place is it, if there's nowhere to hide?"

"It suited me well enough, but now I shall have to find another place," George moaned playfully as he turned to leave but not before he stole a jewel pinned to his sister's elaborately plaited hair and tossed it in the air, his actions daring her to reclaim the jewel.

"Ever the errant child!" she hissed just as playfully and made to go after him.

"And where do you think you're going?" Maud asked as she took Petronelle's arm. The girl's imploring made her mother laugh and the countess released her to go skipping between knights and ladies, servants and yeomen to follow after her brother.

"I'll take what is mine, sir!" she shouted after George, who sped up and raced down to the greater ward. Knights clustered around the standard of the earl of Chester turned and bowed as George arrived at the bottom of the stairs.

"My lord," greeted one knight dressed in new harness that was blazoned with the falcon of Mowbray. He was tall, dark, and extraordinarily handsome, and the rest deferred to him as George approached. No sooner than George was an arm's length from the knight did they laugh and embrace.

"Roger! I heard you'd sailed from Antioch. You are welcome home," George said.

"Gentlemen, this is George, earl of Grasmere, of whom you've heard many stories, and despite his youth, fought well beside the greatest knights in the Holy Land. I owe him my life," Roger Mowbray announced.

"Ten shillings and a girl, if I remember," George

murmured as he accepted the greetings of Chester's men.

"Pardon my lord?"

"I owe you ten shillings and a girl."

"Shall we play for it, my lord?"

"One fall."

George took a sword from one of the squires and waved Roger forward. After a tentative engagement, both men were enjoying the contest, their swords ringing above laughter and encouragement from the knights and soldiers around them, the greater bailey becoming a tournament ground filled with household servants and retainers gathered to cheer George on. For every blow Roger issued, George managed to block and parry, duck or jump out of the way and meet each attack vigorously. But then George recognized an odd sense of foreboding. The light had dimmed and he looked up, searching for clouds, and saw the demon from the market square standing at the end of the yard, towering above the others, watching and laughing. George stumbled and fell. When he sat up on his knees, the crowd erupted in applause and laughter. George glanced around and saw nothing strange or frightening, just his friends and family. Joanna stood on the donjon stairs wrapped in a cloak, her face as pale as the winter sky.

Roger offered a hand and pulled George to his feet.

"Just the ten shillings, George; the girl wasn't worth it," Roger said over the din of applause.

"Am I to suppose that you'll all be bloodied by the time we must go to church?" Petronelle shouted and her words made the men come to attention.

"Roger, you're well acquainted with my sister. She used to write poetry in your honor, didn't she? Perhaps you could be the mysterious knight she's hoping will ride into the church and save her from marriage!"

"George!" Petronelle hissed.

"Well, she's Chester's problem now, God help the bridegroom!" George teased, and was not at all surprised when his sister cursed them and ran back into the donjon.

"Indeed," Roger murmured, watching her retreat.

✠✠✠

EORGE BENT FORWARD and kissed Petronelle's lovely face under the silk veil obscuring her from the rest of the family and the wedding guests. "Shall we go?" he whispered, and patted her hand. Petronelle drew in a ragged breath and nodded, nervously smoothing back a curl that refused to stay under the circlet of jewels that held her veil in place.

George nodded to one of the footmen and the doors to the great hall were thrown back to the shrill of pipes and trumpets. A cheer went up from the family and guests who fell in line and followed Petronelle to the chapel where the rest of the bridal party and the Bishop of Cumbria waited.

The bridegroom, John Harrington, earl of Chester, stood at the door of the chapel with Maud and his own mother, the arrogant beauty called Wendolyne.

"Wendolyne of Chester!" George hissed through his smile. "Nothing would please her more than a grandchild of hers claiming Grasmere! Then she'd have all the land from Carlisle to Ravenscroft."

"I mean to give John nothing but daughters," Petronelle whispered as she nodded and smiled at guests lining the path as she glided by. "Or you shall have to stop bedding every noblewoman in the West Country and West Riding and find a wife to give you a legitimate heir."

"May the saints protect us if all your girls have such spirit."

"Or swoon in disbelief the moment you take a vow of chastity or find a wife."

"First things first: we have to marry you off."

"George . . ."

"Sister?"

"What if I decided not to get married?"

"You should have thought of that when Chester came crawling for your hand."

"What if I came with you? What then?"

They had reached the chapel. Rather than pause before Chester, who smiled broadly and reached for Petronelle, George steered her into the chapel and went through to the sacristy, waving out the bishop and acolytes preparing for mass.

"You can't be serious!" he hissed.

"I decided last night. I will go with you. Why should I always be left at home while you ride off with your vassals and squires to champion honorable causes?"

"The sack of Constantinople was far from honorable! Think of what you're doing."

"I will go with you, George!" Petronelle growled back. "You need someone clever and quick of mind. And if that cold bitch of a princess demands a woman of good breeding and family in her retinue she can accept me—and I will bring Joanna with me as my companion, since you said yourself that she would be better company."

"What's this?"

George looked behind him to see Chester staring up at them. He was a slight man of middle years, but clear of eye and well-made for his short stature. The earl was joined by his imperious mother, who was of the same height as George and perhaps as muscular as he. Maud glided in, slamming the door shut on the curious gathering in the ambulatory. With all eyes on him, George swallowed hard and said, "We may have wasted a great deal of time and money."

"Petronelle?" Maud purred, lifting the veil so that she could see her daughter's face. The voice was to be obeyed. "Darling, what is this?"

"I'm going with George, and that's all that needs to be said," Petronelle gushed, and then took a cautionary step backward.

"No, dearest girl, you're going to be married," Maud said calmly, though George had to take her hand to keep it from trembling more violently than it already was, and to prevent her from striking Petronelle.

"No!!"

"Petronelle, there's not a girl I know that isn't nervous on the day of her wedding," George tried to jest.

"And how would you know? You spurned Elinor Lucy and a hundred more ladies to go on your holy crusade! Be silent, brother!" his sister growled.

Chester took an appraising glance at Petronelle and swallowed hard. "We have an agreement, my lady of Grasmere," Chester addressed Maud without taking his eyes from her daughter. "I could bring you before the king for breach of contract! I could take her by force but I would be in loathe to do so."

"Lord Aumarle of Craven would say otherwise, especially where it concerns his sister Mary," George interjected. He held back Chester with a hand and smiling, added, "I only speak the truth, John. Taking lands is one thing, another man's wife or sister is another. Remember, too, that you are my guest here."

"That doesn't mean I have to stand for insults and humiliation!" Chester said, and placed a hand on the pommel of his sword.

"The marriage contract will be enforced, my lord Grasmere," Wendolyne spoke up, gently pulling her son back.

"It will be. I will talk to my sister and make her see the good reason for it."

"I don't need you to champion me, George. I tell you; I will have my way!" Petronelle demanded.

"And so she shall."

All heads turned at the voice. Aubrey Ascalon stood among them, dressed in his monk's habit. He glanced around at the little crowd and then reached for Petronelle. "I came to celebrate my only daughter's wedding and enter a family quarrel instead. I suppose that's natural in ours. Petra, you look lovely," Aubrey said, kissing her cheek.

"Father," George greeted.

"I think a family council is needed, don't you?" Aubrey asked, smiling faintly.

"Mother, Petronelle, come with me," George

murmured, nodding his head towards the castle. "Father, you also." He turned to Chester and his mother, saying, "We'll only be a moment."

Avoiding all eyes and ignoring the whispers and laughter, George hurried through the throng of guests, dragging a noisily-protesting Petronelle. Maud and Aubrey moved more slowly behind them and chatted with guests as they passed, putting on a good show if anything. Once in the solar with the rest of the family Maud turned on her daughter.

"It's another man, isn't it?" Maud hissed.

"Mother! It's nothing like that. I want to help George."

"In sixteen years you've only just now decided he merits your loyalty?"

"It is what he's called to do. I cannot explain it, Mother. I only know that I have to do this." Petronelle said quietly, yet with passion. "It is my calling, too."

"I didn't come home—" George began, but Aubrey raised a hand to silence him.

"And for that reason I did. She goes with you," Aubrey pronounced.

George slammed his fist on an oak table. "Father, I swear by all that is holy—"

"—that you'll protect your sister," Aubrey interrupted.

"No!" Maud and George exclaimed together.

"You really haven't any choice," said Aubrey.

"Do you think you can come here and make decisions and decree orders after what you've done?" George snapped. "You're not welcome here! I am head of the family now! I am Grasmere!"

"My work is done then," Aubrey said quietly and before he turned to go, he smiled and said, "But your sister will accompany you and that's all there is to say on the matter. *Pax et bonum*."

As quietly as he appeared he was gone.

CHAPTER 8

AUBREY HAD ALREADY entered the stable yard and was going for his mule when he heard the shouts. He paused only for a moment to whisper a prayer of guidance and then spun about, smiling disingenuously for his son, who was hurling towards him like a wild boar.

"I have half a mind to beat you within an inch of your life! What did you think you were doing? You know Petra can't and shouldn't go with me!"

"How do you know?"

"We don't know what lies ahead or who awaits us. I've seen men in the heat of battle. You've seen it. If anything should happen—"

"And you think women could be no different? Given their humors, I should think you'd want an angry girl at your side—especially Petronelle." When George merely frowned, he added, "A little jest."

"Very little!" George sat hard on a bale of hay and put his head in his hands.

"George . . ."

"Why did you do it?"

"We don't have choices."

"Liar! I don't know if it's even possible to keep this bargain you've made."

"You don't have a choice."

"I think I do!"

George glanced up and saw that Aubrey was bending over him, trying to make eye contact. The lovely icon spun on its cord before him. "She was your lover!" George hissed, grabbing the icon.

"No. The only woman I ever loved, the only woman I love now, is your mother," Aubrey said in a husky voice full of emotion.

"Then who is she? Why do you wear it?"

"Go on the quest, George, and you'll have answers to your questions. I cannot give you answers now."

"Why is it that holy men speak in riddles and questions?"

"Farewell, George. Perhaps we'll see one another on your return."

"So easily you come back and just like that you're gone? Don't bother coming round again, Brother!"

"Your anger is the least of our problems right now. Please remember that I love you."

Aubrey took the mule brought forward by a stable boy and easily mounted it. With a blessing, he was gone.

George watched him ride out over the drawbridge and tried to quell the rage that filled his throat. He stalked to the well head and drank, then spat, letting water stain the fine satin of his new surcote. He would have been content to stand there all day had it not been for Chester.

"We had an agreement, Lord Grasmere!" Chester shouted when he was within distance.

"Good God, John, d'you think I don't know?" George grabbed the full bucket on the ledge and plunged his face into it for a moment, then shook his head like a dog.

Chester jumped out of the way. "Gesu Maria! They told me you came back a madman!"

"Who are they?"

"Never mind that! We had an agree—"

"Yes, and we still do."

"And how might that be? Your sister has fantasies of going on a crusade with you for some decaying prince in the north country! A crusade such as Queen Alienor with King Louis of France! And look at the scandal that made!"

George wiped his eyes with the cuff of his linen shirt in order to better see the little man glaring up at him. "Your quarrel is with my father where it concerns the marriage contract. He's just past the blacksmith's; you can catch him up if you run fast enough. Know this one thing, Chester. I am not my father. If I say you have a marriage with my sister, then it will be so. Be patient. You'll have your wife as soon as the circumstances and God will it. We've only postponed the inevitable."

"We have an agreement," Chester repeated, and gripped George's hand. "And I will hold you to it."

"I've no doubt of that, little earl!" George whispered as his eyes followed Chester out of the stable yard.

He was in no mood to confront his mother or sister, nor the imperious and frightening Wendolyne, so George slipped out by way of the postern gate and walked unnoticed towards the south, to a hillock overlooking the castle and Little Langdale, where an ancient oak stood alone. The enormous, gnarled trunk was grooved in just the right angle that a boy or a grown man could tuck himself comfortably into the recess and be hidden from the world to tend to his thoughts and perhaps find quiet.

The Hiding Place.

George eased back against the rough oak bark and watched the clouds pass by overhead at a sluggard's pace towards the lakes where they would empty their snow and sleet by nightfall. How different was this place from the bright, hot landscapes of the Holy Land, the serene Bay of Naples, or the lagoons of Venice.

Twigs snapping made George think that a squirrel or rabbit had come to join him, but he looked over and saw the toe of a leather slipper and the hems of a woolen cloak and a silk gown.

"Good morrow, Joanna," he greeted.

"Pardon, they sent me to find you."

"They, meaning the ladies of the household?"

"Yes, my lord, the same."

"How did you know to come here?"

"I followed you—from a distance—like a stray puppy."

George laughed gently and drew the cloak from around his shoulders, setting it on the ground. He extended a hand and invited her to sit. So you've found my hiding place," he sighed.

"It's not much of a hideaway, is it? All out in the open?"

But when one needs to hide, it's best to do it where no one would expect to look—like out in the open."

Joanna knelt on the cloak and took one of the twigs, tracing in the mud so that the outline of a flower appeared. "How long do you want to hide, my lord?" she said after a time.

"I like you, Joanna; you speak honestly even to the likes of me."

"That's because I'm not much different from you," she replied with a shy smile and a side-long glance that was fleeting and beguiling.

"You see my demons," he murmured.

"Come sir, they wait for you at the castle. The ladies Petronelle and Elinor are screeching at each other like hawks after prey and the countess has closed herself up in the solar. Lord Mowbray thinks you can make them see reason."

George laughed. "Lord Mowbray wishes my sister had not spurned his suit, and as for my ability to make any woman see reason, well . . ."

"I'll speak honestly to the likes of you, George Ascalon," Joanna interrupted. "What if you were to astound everyone and not be who everyone expects you to be? What if you were to be yourself—plain George? As a matter of fact, who is the plain George?"

"Have a care, Mistress Fletcher," George laughed. "You might be mistaken for a lady of gentle breeding or an aesthete. You remind me of the Greek and Italian women, who have a passion for learning and life, and speak openly."

"Shouldn't we all?"

George took up a stick and followed her tracing with it. "Sometimes, often, the passion for life is supplanted by what is expected of us."

"Once a thing is done, it's done. My father heard that said in Italy—in Siena, I think."

He smiled and pushed himself to his feet. "And when it's done, I'll teach you to play chess."

"I know the game, my lord."

"Then we may entertain ourselves while the hawks screech and my saintly mother prays for divine intervention." He offered his hand to Joanna, who took it tentatively and looked down at her shoes when she realized how close he was.

"I have half a mind to kiss you, Joanna," he said softly and caressed her face. She looked up at him and glanced away just as quickly.

"Let it be numbered among my debts to you, my lord!" she whispered, managing a smile.

"He lifted her chin to better see her eyes and said, "Where is the haughty, angry wench from Butcher's Lane? Did you toss her away with the rags on your back?"

"I need no guise here. I believe you have enough regard for me that I may be who I am—plain Joanna," she whispered, their faces close.

"Is this the lady before me?"

She nodded. "What you see before you." As he leaned in to kiss her, Joanna put a finger to his lips. "Let it be numbered among my debts, sir." George smiled back and let go of her, gesturing in the direction of the castle.

✠✠✠

THE SENTRY SHOUTED George's return and he winced as family members and curious guests started out of the donjon to greet him. "Just once I'd like to come and go without such noise and bother!" George grumbled to Joanna, who whispered good bye with an obeisance as she left to follow the women into the bower. "I beg you, stay!" he called.

She turned and glanced first at the women who smiled in that way women did when they 'knew' something, but what did they know? Now she looked at George and would have given in to his mournful, pleading, look had Roger Mowbray not arrived. She knew George and she had been spared the embarrassment of conjecture by this kindly man's intervention.

"Lord Mowbray will have better counsel," Joanna replied and hurried away to join a beckoning Petronelle.

"It's not been a good day for you, my lord," Roger said after greetings were exchanged, "and as I know you have no desire for the interrogations and disapproving looks, the tension that would surely follow while you wrestle with plans everyone expects you to have when in truth you have none—well, I'll be brief. I'm going with you."

George laughed and shook his head. "Ah, no. Your debt to me is paid in full."

"It's true enough, but when have you ever persuaded me to do the opposite of what I intend?"

"There was the matter of my sister."

"Another truth."

"This isn't your pledge, nor quarrel, Roger. You've seen enough in your life without having to do battle once more," George said walking away, though it didn't end the conversation.

"How do you know it's a battle you're facing?" Roger wanted to know as he caught up and followed George into the great hall.

"It is a promise of old made by my father to

another lord. How could it not be?"

"You'll have need of me."

"Roger,"

"My lord, if only to keep you alive - so you can return home and be the country nobleman that you've always dreamt of."

There was no arguing with that.

By the Feast of the Annunciation the roads were clear and all preparations were made. On a chill March morning, George made his farewell his mother and father and led a party that included Petronelle, Roger, Joanna, Richildis, Stephen, and a half-dozen knights out of the castle and northeast to champion Wulfstan, lord of Eskeleth.

✠✠✠

NOTHING AMISS, NOTHING to lose sleep over; thank the angels and saints, so far, so good.

Like the antiphon to a hymn or a prayer the words kept repeating in his mind as George listened to his horse's canter. He glanced behind to his band of pilgrims, then directly to his right at Roger Mowbray, stern-faced and lock-jawed.

"You've got something to say," George hinted when he'd sidled up.

"Don't know what you mean."

"Brow set, eyes in a squint—by all the saints, if you clench your teeth any harder you'll break them!"

Roger shifted slightly and with a mailed hand thumped George on the chest. The movement made George reel a bit and he grabbed the reins tighter to keep himself in the saddle.

"You no sooner return than you are sent on another errand for the honor of Grasmere. Don't you find it all too convenient?"

"No one forced you to come along, Roger."

"Not that; when have I backed away from a challenge? No, it's too convenient. That you are home and these nobles from some hellish place on the moors arrive at the same time with a pledge to be redeemed. Your father has a strange way of punishing you and after all that has happened."

"My father holds many secrets close; this is but one of many."

"From what I know of him – ah, never mind." They rode in silence for a time and then Roger spoke again. "If you must know, I'm here because I fear for the ladies. What madness has taken your lady sister that she should join you on this quest?"

"Strange that you should ask," George quipped. "And that you should come to her wedding. Just how deep is the wound?"

Roger shook his head and urged his horse to keep up with George, who had spurred forward. "War brings all sorts of wounds, my lord. I can only imagine your uncomfortable homecoming with Elinor. For my part, I'm willing to look for a wife elsewhere, since the good lords Mowbray of Osterle and Kenning and earls of Myrce are not good enough for some. Now you," Roger said, clapping George affectionately on the shoulder, "with that pretty face and title, when you return home a hero, you'll have a harvest of brides for the picking, even that delicious waif making eyes at you!"

"Waif?"

"Mistress Fletcher."

George shook his head with a laugh and rode

ahead, uncomfortable with the direction of their
conversation. Friends as he was with Roger, how
could he begin to explain his nights of torment and
horrible dreams and memories, or that the only
person who seemed to dispel these evils was Joanna?
He involuntarily glanced back at the caravan of
soldiers, wagon, and carriage to where Joanna and
Petronelle rode their ponies alongside the carriage.
They were talking and laughing; Petronelle glanced
away when she noticed Roger watched. Joanna,
however, paid no attention to the smiles and greetings
of the household guard and pointed out the beauty of
the landscape before them: the fells and crags of
Cumbria, the shimmering lakes that caught the early
spring sun, and the dappled shadows thrown by the
trees in the forest looming before them. How could
George explain seeking her out in the household, to
watch silently as she plied her needle in the solar or
blended herbs in the drying house; the hours that he
and Joanna spent over games of chess, when nary a
word was spoken and her company was like a
powerful restorative; or how she always seemed to
know when he was the most unhappy and appeared
and managed to bring tranquility just by being there?

Roger would never understand how much more
important now was the stillness of the soul to George
than a patch of land, a purse full of gold coins, or
even someone to warm his bed for a few hours. He
certainly would not accept that Joanna was a cure for
so many ills and none of them of the flesh.

And there was *that* to consider.

What surprised George most was his inaction.
God knew he wanted Joanna, but he also feared that

if he had his wish, something terrible might happen to her or to both of them.

". . . I said, do you want to make camp for the night? We've only an hour left of daylight. George?"

George threw Roger a puzzled glance and nodded absently to his amused smile, ignored the comment that ladies were always good for a daydream.

"Where are we?" Joanna asked, sliding off the saddle as soon as they entered the woods and George sent word down the line to halt.

"My forest of Kentmere. We'll stay the night." George watched as Joanna picked up her skirts and joined the household guard that began unloading tents and started to help pitch them. "Mistress Fletcher!" he called. "What do you think you're doing?"

"Earning my bed and board, sir!" she called back.

"I'd sooner you'd stay with the ladies."

Joanna brushed the hair out of her eyes and frowned, then looked at the soldiers surrounding her. One of them bowed in deference, another nodded his head in George's direction. She dropped the mallet she'd taken up and scuffed through the patches of snow and mud to where George stood.

"It's what I've gotten used to, my lord," Joanna grumbled, "and what people expect of me. After all, I'm the wench from Butcher's Lane, am I not?"

"Well, think of yourself as a lady now," he said gently. "You will dine in our tent this evening."

The early spring sunset was a pink ribbon on the horizon by the time the last of seven tents had been raised and furnished. The greatest of the tents was for George and Roger, the next largest for Petronelle and

Joanna, another for Richildis alone. They were surrounded by four smaller tents for the escort and Stephen. George was seated on a bench having conversation with his men, Stephen, and Roger when Joanna and Petronelle arrived for dinner. The men stood as one and bowed, George coming to greet them. "We keep our chivalry even in the midst of a forest," he said, kissing both women on the cheek. "Petra, you will sit on my left, and Joanna, to my right. I will behave better with such beauty to restrain me."

"Now I understand why Elinor and all your other lovers have fled—no one would believe such drivel!" Petronelle teased and started a ripple of laughter, which continued with more wine and good food well into the night. One of the knights struck up a song on a harp and, while Roger and Petronelle danced, George and Joanna bent over a chessboard. Noticeably absent was Richildis, and this was remarked upon by a number of their party.

"I think it best to leave her alone," Joanna said, pondering a move.

"She's in counsel with the Blessed Virgin and Saint Anne," Petronelle sniffed as she came over for another cup of wine. "And even those ladies she would think unworthy to stand in her presence!"

"How many times has our lady mother told you to show charity and consideration to others, little sister?" George murmured, a pawn suspended over the board. He made ready to place it and paused. "No, I don't think so . . ."

"She'll have you in check," Roger spoke up, joining their circle.

"There are worse things, I think." George set the pawn on a square and Joanna made her move.

"Checkmate!" Petronelle crowed.

"You let me win, my lord. I demand a rematch!" Joanna laughed.

"I demand a kiss," George answered, winking.

"Ah no, sir; that's the wine talking!"

"You owe me at least a kiss for all I've done."

"I fear that one kiss will lead to payment of another kind, and another."

The company began to chant "A kiss!" and clap their hands in rhythm until George leaned in and whispered, "What harm could it do?" He smiled when she nodded demurely and was about to take his reward when suddenly the walls of the tent began to billow like sails and the torches were extinguished by a sudden wind.

"Hey now, what's this?" Roger asked, and went to the flaps to look outside.

Gusts of wind were throwing a spring snowfall into flurries and whipping them into spirals and fantastic shapes. Nothing more would have been thought of it until one of the shapes took a human, ghostly form in great, billowing robes made of blue and pale gold flame and started moving towards the tent. A low, guttural moan replaced the wind shrieking in the trees and grew louder, painful to the ear, and then became a three-note cadence plucked on a harp, keeping time with the beating of their hearts. The spirit moved slowly, not touching the ground, but gliding and spinning in and out of the trees. Roger and George drew their swords, as did the rest of their knights.

"Stay with the women," George said to Stephen, and pushed him towards the back of the tent.

The armed contingent went outside where they discovered three more of the apparitions hovering above the ground. The moon had come from behind the clouds and its light on the snow made George think they had an advantage until the first of the ghostly creatures attacked. The screams were terrifying, making him forget for a moment the bone-chilling and paralyzing cold that overwhelmed him when the creature seemed to pass through him as if George was made of air. When he regained his senses, warmth took over and he was able to raise his sword arm—to no avail. He attacked again, and as George cleaved one of the creatures in two, it melded back into another shape, this of a great winged serpent with fiery eyes and tongue of flames of many different colors. The creature lunged at George and he felt a searing pain, cold yet not cold; hot, but freezing. He felt nausea and a burning sweat as he continued to fight, slashing at the ghostly beast and missing his mark time and again, as if he were swinging at nothing, or the air. Just as he thought he was going to perish, George noticed the woman standing in the midst of the battlefield. It was Joanna.

"Stay . . . back!" George struggled to shout. His movements were slower and heavier, and it was like cutting through porridge as the beast swirled, dived, and then suddenly turned, heading for Joanna.

George and Roger both hurled themselves toward her and were amazed when a flurry blinded them. Just as suddenly as they had come, the storm and the apparitions were gone. Joanna was nowhere to be seen, but Richildis came from her tent and looked perturbed by the commotion. She glared at the men and went back inside.

"Whatever they were, they're gone," Roger panted. He leaned forward to rest his hands on his knees, trying to catch his breath.

The men found themselves alone in a silent snowfall, the countryside tranquil and beautiful. George pitched his sword into a new drift and looked around at his startled and exhausted men. He saw Petronelle and Joanna watching from the tent flap.

"I hold no one to my father's promise," George announced. "We see that this is no ordinary battle. Those of you who do not wish to accompany me have leave to return to your homes with my good will and thanks—or perhaps it would be better if you did."

One by one, voices rose.

"No my lord, I am with you!"

"I stand for God and Grasmere!"

"It is for the honor of Grasmere I do come!"

One oath he heard above all the others. George swallowed the lump rising in his throat when he saw Petronelle take up a sword from a knight and heard her cry, "I go with my brother! For God and Grasmere! The honor of Ascalon!"

CHAPTER 9

N OTHING WAS SAID of the strange night.
George walked alongside the carriage trying
to make pleasant conversation with Richildis,
leading his horse by the reins. She responded absently
to his inquiries and made no eye contact, and finally
George admitted defeat, mounting up and riding
forward to catch up with Roger and their men.

"I told you, there's something not right about that
one. I think she had something to do with it." Roger
murmured. "Strange things happen when she's
around. I've heard tell that there are women of the
north who practice the old ways; they know the dark
arts."

"Are you calling her a witch?" George scoffed.

"Or something like it, though you could put the
letter 'b' where the 'w' is and have something
altogether different, and perhaps closer to the truth."

"She certainly has no care for chivalry," George
said, looking back at the carriage.

"You cannot fault a man for trying," Petronelle
spoke up, joining them.

"Don't you start!" her brother grumbled.

"I'm not criticizing you, George," she continued.
"You have shown the lady every courtesy and every
kindness, observed the rules of chivalry, and she
treats you as if you were nothing more than that
squirrel in the tree."

"At least squirrels get an acorn or a pine nut from a gentle hand," Roger quipped.

"You were well fed, my lord!" Petronelle snapped at him.

"And as quickly as you offered, you took away!" said Roger between his teeth.

George sighed and urged his horse forward, eager to leave Kentmere Forest and not be brought into an old quarrel he had grown tired of. His spirits lifted when they came out and continued northeast, a journey uneventful and silent until they reached the outskirts of Kendal on the border between Cumbria and the west riding of Yorkshire. Roger had stopped arguing with Petronelle and muttered something about preferring ghosts to highway-men as he drew his sword.

George now looked in the direction of Roger's sword point where, on the northern road, was an overturned cart and several people clustered around it trying to salvage what they could of its bounty. Off to the side was a dead horse and, further still, a knight lying in a ditch. Before George had a chance to survey the situation, Roger was thundering up the road, shouting at the Grasmere host to follow.

"My lord Grasmere?"

George wheeled his horse about and trotted back to the carriage. "There's trouble afoot, milady," George answered Richildis' inquiry.

"Mowbray rushed to play the champion," Richildis sniffed, and George felt her words and eyes making a foul assessment.

"And too foolishly! *Wealdgengan!*" George hissed, reaching for his sword. What had the promise of a rescue mission was now an ambush, as a rag-tag band of thieves, called *Wealdgenga*— worthless, landless, men disowned by their families, some of them deserters from the Crusades—dropped from trees and came out of the forest to engage this new band of travelers. George charged.

"Will you leave us at the mercy of those who mean to do harm?" Richildis cried. No sooner had she said this than the two knights guarding the carriage were struck down by arrows shot from the trees.

"Bring the carriage into the woods!" Joanna shouted at its driver. "You! Take the cart and follow!" she yelled at the squire leading the supply cart. Rather than do as bid, both fled into the woods. Joanna turned to Stephen who had gone the color of whey and now looked as if he would be ill.

"Surely you know how to use a sword!" Joanna snapped at him.

"It would be best to leave such things to true men at arms!" Stephen gasped and fell out of the carriage in his haste to find a place to be sick. As soon as he had emptied his stomach, another brace of *Wealdgenga* came upon them and he ran, screaming for mercy.

"My lady! Follow with the carriage!" Joanna screamed at Richildis who was trying to disembark and follow Stephen.

"Look to it yourself! I am no ambler or camp follower!" she hissed, but before she could retreat back into the safety of the carriage, Petronelle responded with a litany of oaths and dragged the screaming woman out and pulled her along to the safety of the woods. Joanna rode up and as quickly as she dismounted she bounded into the supply cart and followed the other women. Once they were far enough from the melee, Joanna drove to a halt and turned to scavenge the bales and sacks of supplies, pulling out an iron pot and two knives.

"Take these!" Joanna ordered, shoving the pot at Richildis, the knife at Petronelle.

"How will this protect me, pray?" Richildis demanded.

"A good, swift blow to the head," Joanna answered as she led them to the shelter of a large oak. "I supposed Petronelle knows how to use a knife, that it wouldn't be beneath her station and duty to use it!" she added when Richildis looked about to protest.

"Stand ready!" Petronelle warned, pointing beyond the trees where thieves approached the carriage, looked about and then came towards them. Just as one man came around the tree, Joanna surprised him with a plunge of the knife into his side. Petronelle finished him off and shoved Richildis behind her, acting as a shield from the next thief, tripped up by Joanna as he tried to grab at them. Joanna put her knife into his groin and then swiped the blade across his throat.

No one else approached as they crouched, waiting. The sounds of fighting up the road echoed through the woods, sending fear through Joanna as she listened and prayed, clutching her knife in readiness. "We did well for ourselves, Mistress Joanna! We've cheated my brother out of a good fight," Petronelle said happily. She wiped a smear of blood from Joanna's cheek and then clasped her trembling hand.

"There's no one left. We should go back to the carriage," Richildis spoke up. "We'll be safer there."

"That is doubtful, but at least we could ride off. Come then," Joanna remarked and led the way back.

"We would have been safer here," Richildis sniffed when they were enclosed in the confines of the carriage and she was bundled in fur robes, curled up on cushions in a far corner. "How fortunate you didn't get us killed!"

"And I suppose it would have been better to let them take us for ransom or worse!" Joanna snapped in return. "You asked for good women to accompany you; be glad those women know how to use weapons with good courage!"

"Do you speak to me as if you were my equal, girl?"

Joanna was ready to snipe but Petronelle shook her head and drew Joanna close so they could watch and wait.

On the road, George was battling a huge brute of a man who was scarred from ear to ear and lacked half of his nose. Every blow the giant threw at George vibrated through his body as their swords met. He nearly tripped over the body of one of his knights but found his footing and managed to strike blow after blow with renewed energy until he'd cornered the giant against an oak. The giant threw a blow with a mailed fist at George's stomach and he staggered backwards into a roadside ditch, trying to get his breath. For a moment, George thought he would lose consciousness, and he watched as Roger killed the last of the *Wealdgengan*.

But it was the giant that held George's vision—

the large face and torso was changing before his eyes.
Where once an ugly, battle-scarred soldier stood,
there now was a gentleman all in dark purple, with a
purple hood, a circlet of gold on his head. His face
was obscured, and in the light it was hard to tell the
features. For one moment, George thought it was his
father; the next, himself; and again, his father. But the
eyes were dead and there was something mesmerizing
about him. George was so enthralled by this new
opponent that he dropped his sword and waited. He
would have been cleaved in two by a battle ax the
assailant easily swung over his head had Roger not
come forward and run him through the back with
George's sword. George pulled himself up and stared
down at the dying *Wealdgengan.*

"Our thanks to you both!" cried a gentleman as
he crept from a hiding place. "That we should be so
fortunate in travelers upon the road – ah! My lord
Grasmere!"

He doubled over in a bow and George's brows
arched at his familiarity, recognizing him then as one
of the travelers he'd seen in the common room at
Deadman's Last in Grasmere.

"Are you all unharmed?" George queried, looking
around for the rest of his party.

"We are sound, praise be to God. My young lord
will give you something for your trouble if you wish
it. Adam! Adam, come forward and offer tribute."

A boy ran to join them, a bloodied sword in hand
and a dazed but satisfied grin on his face. "Thomas,
did you see it? I killed two of them! They were
deserters from the Crusades, weren't they?" Adam
Middleton stopped when he saw George and nodded

curtly, one lord to another. "It was you who came to our aid? Did you know these men, my lord?"

"I don't know if they were crusaders. Besides, how would I know every man who takes up crusade? Every man I knew and loved died in Constantinople." George said, walking away. "And these men will have mothers and wives to mourn them. What valor is in that?" He turned suddenly on the boy. "Or do you still think me a coward?" George asked bluntly, leveling his sword. "The next time you make such an accusation, you ought to have better proof than lies and gossip from those who never set a foot out of Grasmere! Get out of my way."

Adam sprinted after him and threw himself in George's path. "I owe you my life!" he cried.

"Get up. Paid in full, Middleton of Gawthorp. Go home and be a comfort to your mother."

As George whistled for his horse and began walking back to the caravan, Adam bolted after him. "Let me come with you! I'm as good as my father!" the boy cried.

"I've no doubt of that, and I'm sure you'd tell me differently if I thought otherwise," George responded, picking up speed with the hope of losing Adam. His knights formed a guard around him but Adam managed to get through and once again threw himself in George's path.

"I tell you, I'm as good as my father! What must I do to prove myself?" Adam demanded, his voice wavering.

"Do as you're told—that's the true measure of a man; to show obedience no matter how difficult or unworthy the cause. I know what I'm speaking of,

Adam. Now go; you're all your mother has in the world to protect her against those who would take the Gawthorp honors for themselves," George answered.

"I have a brother not yet seven."

"You'd leave your mother to a child? Adam, great men do not act so foolishly. No, your mother needs you by her side."

"My father's—my manor is not a day's ride away. You can ask her yourself," Adam pronounced.

"I have a pledge to honor, and I'd sooner redeem myself and not delay—God's wounds, what's this?" George said, and stopped short when he saw the bodies lying outside the carriage. He signaled to his men for quiet and to draw their swords. They crept upon the carriage and as George whipped aside the curtains, he was met with screams and the point of Joanna's knife.

"By the saints! I might have killed you!" Joanna shrieked at him. "You ought to know better— announce yourself next time!"

"Is anyone hurt?" George demanded.

"We're whole, and saints be praised, the lady Richildis' virtue is still intact," Petronelle answered, pulling a silly face at her brother that was unseen by Richildis.

"Now my lady Petronelle, that was unkind," Roger tut-tutted.

"No more than the truth," Richildis sniffed as she retreated deeper into the furs and cushions to stare out the window.

"Nothing could breach that wall of frost and ice," muttered Joanna and she received raised brows and a shake of the head from George. "It's what you've been thinking," she added with another shrug.

"Are you all right?" George asked softly, taking the knife from her.

Joanna nodded and began smoothing her hair, wiping blood from her hands and the sleeves of her dress, glancing at the men nervously. "I suppose now you'll scold and tell me it's not the way a lady behaves—Lord, look at me! One might think I spent all morning in a butcher's stall; surely you're not accustomed to ladies mired in blood . . ."

"I'm not accustomed to ladies with such courage," he whispered.

"My lord?" Adam spoke up. "I think this lady and all present deserve a quiet night in a safe and protected place, such as Gawthorp. What say you?"

George nodded and waved over one of the knights, never taking his eyes from Joanna. "Send a man ahead to tell Lady Middleton that her son and his companions ask her hospitality. And send someone to find Stephen and the others and if they're still alive, then arrange for the burial of the dead."

"These thieves and murderers?" Richildis demanded.

"Surprise us by showing a charitable side, Lady Richildis," George said as he walked away with his men to their horses. He stopped Joanna as she lit from the carriage to find her pony.

"Please, no chiding," Joanna begged, waving him off. "I was taught to defend myself along with the sewing and cooking."

"I give this into your care."

Joanna turned and saw that he held out the sword of Ascalon. "What's this?" she asked.

"I can think of no one better to keep it safe, and no one better it should protect."

She tried not to bow under its weight, but Joanna smiled nevertheless and carried it carefully to her pony, tucking it into the saddle bag. Her heart pounded as if he'd made a declaration of love.

✠ ✠ ✠

GAWTHORP MANOR WAS a house, a farm, a chapel, cluster of cottages, and the ruins of a Norman castle held up with scaffolding, the repairs abandoned years ago. Nothing to be impressed with, George thought to himself as he dismounted in the stable yard and looked about.

A boy peered out from the doors of a barn and watched George with a frown set from brow to chin. That glowering look grew darker when the rest of the Ascalon party clattered into the yard, Adam Middleton with them.

"Adam! Adam!" the boy shrieked and risked life and limb to reach him. Roger cursed when the child got in the way of his lathering stallion and was nearly thrown from the saddle trying to avoid injury to the boy and himself.

"Mind where you run, boy!" George shouted, grabbing the child, who squirmed and wriggled like an anxious puppy.

"Martin, do as you're told!" Adam had dismounted and was now striding across the yard.

"You lied to me!" Martin shrieked. "You said I could go with you to Wales! I woke and you were gone and Mother said it was no good to fret over what couldn't be!" After this tirade, he kicked Adam soundly in the shin and then took a jab at his stomach. George and Roger grabbed Adam before he doubled over and helped him to a bale of new hay where he sat until he recovered his wind.

"This . . . is my . . . welcome home!" Adam wheezed. "I should . . . take a rod . . . to your backside!"

"You lied!" Martin wailed now and stood as the hub in a circle of adults while he sobbed. Petronelle clucked her tongue and knelt down to face the child, putting her hands on his shoulders as he convulsed with hiccups.

"There, Martin! Why do you fret? Your brother is home and is glad to see you. You've had to care for this great household, while he's done nothing more than get a sore backside from riding a horse for days. Now, I've never met your lady mother; do you suppose I might have that honor? I've heard she is no less than a queen."

Martin wiped his eyes with the backs of his grimy hands and nodded, looking at Petronelle suspiciously. After a moment he nodded again and tried a smile. "Are you a queen?" he whimpered between hiccups.

"Of certain hearts, I think," George quipped, letting his eyes slide towards Roger.

A door nearly burst off its hinges as the household poured out. Behind them like a clucking mother hen was a large woman in plain clothes, wearing a tarnished circlet on her veil and wimple.

"At last!" the woman cried with delight. "Adam! We have waited so long—and you've brought a proud company with you! I hope there will be enough to feed and board everyone."

"Mother, this is George Ascalon, earl of

Grasmere, and his retinue, among them the fair
Richildis of Eskeleth," Adam greeted, sweeping his
hands in the direction of the party.

Lady Middleton's eyes flickered a bit and she
nodded to the woman climbing down from the
carriage. The household staff bowed as one.

"We ride north to Arkengarthdale, called by Lord
Wulfstan to honor a promise. We will only stay the
night, Madam, and then continue on our way,"
George explained. "Here is my sister, Lady Petronelle
Ascalon, espoused to the earl of Chester, and our
friend, Joanna Fletcher. And Roger Mowbray, late
knight of the king's household and now lord of
Osterle and Kenning and earl of Myrce. Here I do
present the fair Richildis, as Adam rightly calls her."

Another ripple of bows and deferential
murmuring swept the household.

"We shall not keep you a moment longer than
necessary. Come in, Lord Grasmere, and refresh
yourself and your following," Lady Middleton purred.
She extended a hand and George led her into the
manor on his arm.

The great hall looked more like a shed than the
room of state it was meant to be. Plank boards were
set on trestles and two chairs of state were placed at
the center of one. Dogs sniffed about in the rushes,
and pigeons flew in and out of a window, driving the
servants to distraction while they cleaned up from the
aftermath of a banquet, scooping up battered cups of
silver and knives, bowls, and flagons that had seen
better days. The roof leaked and the fire in the pit
hissed when water drops fell. There were no
decorations in the room to prove that this was the

manor of the lords of Gawthorp.

"I see that the Crusades have made you poorer, lady," George commented. "Was everything sold to ransom your eldest son?"

"You know the story so I needn't tell it," Lady Middleton replied. "Much good that came of the effort and sacrifice—dying as he did on the voyage from Messina. Come this way; I have chambers above stairs that you may use. The household is reduced to nothing these days. I've lost two sons and a husband to crusade and I fear there will be more." She nodded in Adam's direction.

George noticed the look borne of hope and trepidation on Adam's face and he studied the boy a moment before saying, "There may be a way to prevent that, my lady."

"Short of sending my youngest sons to a monastery for safekeeping, I think not."

"I am in need of a squire on this quest of mine," George said. "To say the truth, Adam offered his service to me, but knowing his family, I would not have it. Now I see he would fare better on our crusade in the dales than to any in the Holy Land."

"Thank you, my lord!" Adam cried with delight and backed away when he saw his mother's face.

"What say you, Madam? I can give you his wages in advance—ten gold angels?"

"Ten! Mother! That would be more than enough to patch the roof, and lay new slate stones in the hall and buy back your jewels and plate!" Adam gushed. Again, he backed away upon seeing the hard set of his mother's tightly pursed mouth. "Arkengarthdale is not as far away as Jerusalem," he muttered.

"Forgive me," George apologized. "I should not have presumed when you offer such hospitality."

"Who am I to turn away generosity?" she sighed. "It is ever a mother's duty to say farewell to her sons as they make their way in the world," And saying this, she bestowed a kiss on her eldest surviving child's brow. "It shall be as my lord of Grasmere says. Adam, you will show your liege lord and his company to their chambers. I will see to our supper."

Up two flights of stairs the manor house was in better condition and the rooms better appointed. Once alone in a bedchamber, George listened to the closing of doors and the conversations behind them until the only sounds came from the kitchens below. He kicked off his boots and lay down on the plump featherbed bubbling over the chests it sat upon. The sheer luxury of a soft bed in a house gave rise to contentment, and he relaxed, closing his eyes. He dreamt of his last day in Constantinople. George found himself dressed in full harness as he wielded the Sword of Ascalon against knights sent to kill him. So arrayed, it ought to have been an easy task to vanquish men he thought had been his companions in arms, his brothers, as they destroyed, looted, and raped the fair city of the East.

One knight came for George with a broadsword as long as his arm. George attacked but his assault did nothing, not even a dent in the shield. He was being pushed backwards by their engagement and found himself in a narrow lane against a row of houses still smoldering from fires. It was then he saw the baby sitting in a courtyard and tried to reach him, the knight's blows making it impossible to advance as

George countered each attack as he moved backwards into the courtyard. He fell and rolled towards the fountain, trying to grab the child. The knight stood over him, sword held high and ready. George waited for the end, but it did not come, not then. A lovely woman in diaphanous linen robes appeared out of the smoke and revived him with life-restoring kisses. He tried to brush back her hair to look at her face, but it was obscured by a golden light pouring from the clouds and mist that had come with the dawn . . .

George woke, sweating and trembling, looking about in fear, not remembering where he was. The moon was shining in the bedchamber, and he heard laughter and song somewhere in the distance.

"My lord?"

Joanna's face was visible in the flame of a single candle.

"Supper is laid, and the musicians have struck a tune—the whole village has come to take meat and drink with you. Your sister and the Lady Richildis— something is wrong! I'll call for a physician—"

George grabbed her hand to prevent her from leaving. "No; only restlessness and weariness—how they come to be one, I don't know," he lied, taking the candle from her and placing it on the bed table.

"You look feverish,"

"Only a dream."

"Will you come to supper, then?"

"In a moment."

"I'll leave you to your preparations," she said, going to the door.

"No, stay. Keep me company for a while—I'm not ready to receive the accolades and blessings of complete strangers," George muttered.

Joanna sat nervously on the stool by the bed, making a great effort to smooth her gown and pull the sleeve cuffs down over her hands, tidying the cuffs of her linen shirt.

"If you're in a hurry to go—"

"I know you find my company tiresome, my lord; I'm a stray puppy, I think is what you said."

"A puzzling lady, more like!"

Joanna looked towards the door when there was a burst of laughter and applause downstairs. "I suppose they'll want to honor their hero soon; you did battle valiantly."

"Any man would have done the same." George watched the candle flame dance in the draft from the windows and then studied the silhouette Joanna made against the threadbare tapestry covering the wall, noticing the graceful curves. "And certain women. Were you as afraid as I?"

Joanna turned, the surprise apparent on her face and George smiled involuntarily, her beauty never more apparent to him than now.

"You were fearful? I cannot believe that!"

"Every time I go into battle . . . but you showed strength of courage that would be admirable in any proven knight—as if it were nothing. I would find it hard to believe that any horror should creep into your life, if I didn't know it already had."

"There is more," Joanna said faintly.

"Tell me."

"I do not think it would interest you."

"Are we not friends now? Your secrets are mine."

"I think another time, when the tasks before you are inconsequential."

"Nothing in my life is inconsequential—except me."

"One day you'll not care so much about what others have led you to believe about yourself, and it will do you a world of good."

George slid off the bed and came around to where she stood and gently drew her closer, catching a scent of rosemary and lavender as she moved. The soft wool of her surcote was downy soft against his rough palm, as was her cheek. "How does a fletcher's wife from Butcher's Lane, who should only care about her own life and survival, care so much about another's soul?" he wondered.

During the interval before she spoke, a light breeze made the tendrils of hair dance beneath her coif, the candle flame spark and bob. She listened to the music from below stairs and stared at the hem of her gown and the scuffed toes of her slippers, knowing he waited for an answer. Joanna swallowed hard and sighed.

"It comes when she is born the daughter of the lord earl of Merioneth and the lady of Gwynedd, and through misfortune she is forced to make her way like a camp follower or leman; she learns that titles and lands mean slavery if one is a woman and heiress—and that is all I'll tell you for now."

It came out as a rush of wind so that he could barely perceive what she'd said in such in hurry. When it sank in, George stared incredulously at her, as if seeing a lady altogether different, and he moved away from her, shaking his head.

"I should not have said what I did," Joanna began, but George knelt before her and kissed the hems of her gown, and looked up at her after doing so.

"I pledge my life to you, my lady!" he whispered. Joanna gasped and moved away, taking back her gown. "I am bound by the code of chivalry—"

"You insult me!"

And with that, Joanna swept out of the chamber, banging the door behind her. George sat back on his knees, wondering what just had happened, an apology left wasted on his lips.

CHAPTER 10

I T LOOKED INDEED as if the whole of the countryside had assembled at Gawthorp Manor, for there wasn't a spare inch of free space or air in the great hall. Seated at the high table were Petronelle, Roger, Richildis, Stephen, and the Middletons, who were holding court and deep in their cups. Musicians struck a tune, a country dance, and revelers got to their feet. The thump of feet and hands marking time was like a heartbeat.

As soon as George came downstairs cheers went up and he was clapped heartily on the back and his hand shaken until he felt as if it would drop off. When he finally took the only empty chair at the high table, it was beside Richildis, and George was in no mood to endure her indifference and scorn. He was weary and wanted to go back to sleep, nightmares be damned.

"Do you not enjoy the tribute, my lord?" Richildis asked, offering her cup.

"A poor excuse to waste food and expense in bad times," George remarked, signing he did not wish to drink. "When I return home, I'll see that all are provided for, great and low."

"My brother is of the noble kind, Lady Richildis," Petronelle spoke out, pouring a cup of wine. "He was

disappointed that his crusade led to dismal failure."
Taking another drink she began to laugh. "He is
forever a champion to those in need, though the one
in greatest need is himself!"

"Eskeleth affords him nothing but honor, and we
long to give him tribute," said Richildis, holding up a
bowl of dates for George to savor. He tasted a few
and wiped his hands on a towel, saying, "Perhaps the
lady Richildis would honor me with a dance? I would
count that as a tribute."

"No matter his crusades or failures, Lady
Petronelle, your brother speaks well for himself,"
Richildis said over her shoulder as they joined the
dancers.

Usually clumsy on his feet, George was more so
while dancing with Richildis. Every movement she
made was musical and sensual, while he stumbled
about and forgot steps, feeling as if he was drunk.
Expecting a biting remark or worse, George was
amazed when she smiled and said, "You have the
look of one who would be more comfortable putting
his demons to rest rather than dance."

The comment made him pause, and the dancers
behind him hurried to get out of the way. "Why
would you say that?" George asked.

"You have the world-weary look of one who has
seen terrible things and cannot forget."

They stepped off again, gliding now through a
basse danse, the strains of the music measured by
tambor and pipes. Again, George found it difficult to
move with any grace. "Since you have a gift of
prophecy and sight, tell me," he murmured.

"You have demons of your own, yet you are

called to champion my father because of a promise made."

"Well said. Let that be the end of it."

"As you will."

"I marvel at your change of temper where it concerns me, my lady," George said as they came together in the dance.

"When troubadours sing of the valor of knights, it makes one wary while in their company, not having seen the accomplishments praised. I cannot say the same of you. You proved your courage today."

"I'm glad I could please you, for I was beginning to think that winning your favor would be my greatest challenge!" he said half in jest.

"That remains to be seen."

The familiar chill in her voice returned, as did the icy glance from her beautiful eyes. Her hands were growing colder as the dance continued, though the room was warm and choking with smoke from the cresset lamps and hearth, so cold that they seemed to burn. George let go hastily when the music ended and found an excuse to speak with Adam. He knew Richildis was watching him; that painful, uncomfortable sensation of someone's eyes burning into his back was never more apparent than now. When he turned to greet another guest begging his favor, George saw Joanna standing apart from the others, staring down into her goblet of wine as if it was the most interesting thing in the room. Before he realized what he was doing, George was standing over her, his hands trembling and his mouth dry, and every sensation heightened by her presence.

She resumed the vigil on her cup while he stared.

"Have I grown a wart, sir?" she asked tartly, waiting.

"Here I do humbly beg your pardon, Joanna," he confessed.

"You are forgiven, my lord," she murmured, looking off to the side, at dancers' feet, anywhere but his face.

"A knight's greatest honor is not on the battlefield, but to be worthy of the esteem and affection of a lady," George said, bringing her close. His words were slurred and heavy though why, he did not know. He'd had no great amount of wine that night.

"And how more fearful is a woman's scorn than the horrors of battle!" Joanna quipped, attempting to smile. "Wine often steels courage and I think you have had enough courage for ten men!"

"I need no wine. I owe you a kiss," he whispered. "You may not think it, but you brought me out of a slumber that was near to killing me, and so—"

George paused only for a moment and kissed her gently. He lifted her chin to study her pretty face and saw neither fright nor repugnance. A gentle finger traced the outline of her neck and slid along the cord that held a small jewel, letting it rest on the stone as it gently rose and fell between her breasts.

"Your speeches are pretty enough, and I liked your kiss," Joanna whispered, her face close enough for him to take another taste of her lips. "But I think all this poetry is wasted on me."

George, though taken aback, didn't move. "And why, Mistress, would you think that?"

"I've heard it said that George Ascalon loses his heart for only as long as he's in a lady's bed, and he's not come to my bedchamber door. Though I wouldn't know what to do or say if he did."

"I won't deny that I find pleasure in the hunt for the true mistress of my heart."

"For now you must keep your father's promise, and put all else aside."

George took her hand as she turned to leave. "And if I prove my worth to you?"

"The quest at hand, my lord," she insisted in a gentle voice and turned to applaud the dancers as they finished the measure.

For the rest of the evening George played at dice with Roger and Adam, avoiding the stares that Richildis sent his way, stole glances at Joanna when he thought no one else saw, and tried to shake the puzzling disorientation beginning to overwhelm his senses. He waited until his purse was empty and the ladies had gone up before he said good night to Adam and his mother and made for his own bed.

There were no servants to spare and so George found his way in the dark without the help of a torch. Up the stairs and to the right, as he remembered it. Strangely enough, the door was stuck or locked. George fumbled with the latch but the door wouldn't budge. He thumped against it and pushed until it opened with the aid of Joanna's hand.

"My lord?" Joanna greeted, reaching out to help George break his fall.

"How did you come to be in my room?" he gasped.

"But it's my chamber, sir!" she laughed.

"Ah, so I've knocked upon my lady's bedchamber door."

He was given a kiss full on the mouth, passionate and telling. Rather than waste words on chivalry or courtesy, George returned the kiss and in moments they were tumbling on the featherbed, groping at clothes and struggling to be free of them, laughing when one of the gold buttons on George's surcote was torn from the breast and extinguished a candle in its flight. Kisses were planted haphazardly and promises and endearments whispered in husky tones, things lovers do in the heat of a tryst. Gone were the horrors of the battlefield for George; the visions of a city in flames and the screams of women and children. All that mattered was Joanna.

George lay quietly with her nestled in his arms. "Joanna?" he whispered, bussing her ear. "Love?"

"Mmmmm?" The sigh was contented.

"I promise you, you're no light love, Joanna. When we return to Grasmere, we'll have things set properly — I'll search out your father and settle on any dowry he asks, so long as you are mine and I am yours!"

Joanna's laugh sounded strange, almost like a growl. George opened his eyes and was about to ask what was amiss when he flung himself out of bed. Richildis lay among the tangle of bedclothes.

She stretched seductively, languorously; her ravishing body naked before him, Richildis beckoned George return to bed. Her laughter increased as he backed away, pulling on his clothes, until it was almost a hiss. Before George's eyes she began to transform. Her pale, white skin began to turn to golden scales and her eyes glowed darker until they were like rubies; her golden hair was replaced by

layers of scales and before George was a monstrous
serpent.

The beast lunged, spewing sulfur and fire from its
throat, lashing out with its tail. George threw himself
out of harm's way and hid behind furniture while
looking frantically for a weapon, anything to protect
himself. He saw the sword he'd given into Joanna's
keeping—that glimmer in the far corner away from
the door was a lifesaving beacon.

George crawled on his stomach to grab the
sword, flames shooting over his head and
surrounding him. He pulled the table over and
knocked it on its side to use as a shield while making
futile attacks and the beast coiled and lunged to
counter his every movement. Had the floor not given
way, George would have perished in the jaws of the
beast. He fell in at a sickening, painfully slow pace,
spiraling downwards until he found himself in the
Great hall of the manor, where the room was
illuminated by a full moon that had escaped from
storm clouds. A dog was foraging in the rushes for
bones and servants lay on pallets, snoring softly. The
only smoke came from the cooling embers of a fire
long extinguished.

"Something wrong, my lord?"

George lifted his head from the table, wiped the
ale from his face. A servant stood over him, a torch in
his hand. "Did you —?" George sputtered, looking
around. Just a dream, nothing more, he assured
himself.

"Your lady sister said to leave you where you were
sleeping," the servant offered. "Begging your pardon,
sir, but Lady Middleton's ale is strong for most. If

you'd like, I'll light your way to bed."

"Yes, please," George said and shoved away from the table, stepping carefully around the others sleeping in their places. Once in his room, he fell into a troubled sleep and did not wake until Roger pounded on his door at dawn, saying it was time to go. George was ready to forget the nightmare until he saw Richildis in the stable yard. There was a knowing flicker in her eyes, a telling, evil look.

As she boarded the carriage, she opened her hand and let the sunlight catch a golden button sitting in her palm.

CHAPTER 11

I WONDER IF THIS is how the Israelites felt when they beheld the land of milk and honey."
Roger sidled up beside Joanna and looked off in the distance to where she pointed, offering a sideways grin as she did so. "A cruel jest that, Mistress!" he replied.

Under the dense clouds that turned pewter and grayish-green as eastern winds picked up, the Grasmere party looked upon a vale in Yorkshire, a place that once held the promise of beauty, but now lay in waste. The walls of Eskeleth rising out of the valley were pale and glowing with streaks of sunlight that pierced the leaden sky. All was still, and despite the first signs of spring and the showings of new growth and greenery in the dales as they came from the west, there was no renewal here but rather something strange and foreboding. Stranger still was the massive keep and towers of Wulfstan's castle. Although everything was colorless and dead, the towers, spires, and walls of the Golden Tower were just that—they glowed as if hammered out of a smith's forge, like a beacon to travelers. Great clouds of steam and fog rode from the stone of the town walls and lie heavily on the roofs of Eskeleth; the climate was humid and near suffocating.

George peeled off his cloak and unfastened the

gorget he wore, wiping his sweating face with the cuff of his sleeve. "Lady Richildis!" he called behind him; "we've arrived."

"Perhaps too late!" Adam murmured. "What do you think, my lord? Death seems to be everywhere."

George led his party forward into the vale and past fields once bountiful and rich with grain, pastures upon which cattle and sheep once grazed, now scorched and blackened, past the charred remnants of villages and farms. By the time they arrived at the western gate of the town, a storm broke, and it was no ordinary storm.

Where there ought to have been sleet and rain, or even snow in this northern corner of England, the rain felt as hot as bathwater, and it stank of sulfur like Greek fire. The stench was thick and putrid.

George wheeled about and rode back to the carriage. "Is it always like this?" He demanded of Richildis.

"Since the days of my grandfather Harold; and now you know why my father asked Grasmere to honor its pledge," Richildis answered in a sullen, sonorous voice, like one drugged by poppy juice.

"And you think Grasmere can turn about what the Lord God has done to this place?" George laughed.

"This was never God's doing."

George glanced sideways at Richildis and saw a red glint in her eyes for a just a moment. He turned sharply to look directly at her and now saw a dull, lifeless gaze.

"You truly expect a miracle if you think I can cure your ills! I have half a mind to turn round and go back to Cumbria!"

"You will not; you know it would be impossible."

"Impossible is the task set before me!"

"Take ease, brother; we've come this far," Petronelle urged.

Stephen then gave the order to halt, which only piqued George's anger. "Who are you to give orders to my men and party?" he snapped.

"My lord!" Stephen called, scrambling out of the carriage. "My lord, you must now send your host away—back to Cumbria! They cannot come with you. And this carriage and provisions—they will do you no good here."

"Must we walk the rest of the way?" asked Petronelle.

"We'll suffocate in this dank rain!" Joanna added.

"It is part of the conditions agreed upon," Stephen told them.

"Am I allowed to keep two seconds?" George demanded.

"Only two."

"Roger, Adam; stay with us," George called.

"No! The horses return to Cumbria," Stephen said as they rode forward. Roger and Adam dismounted and took their saddles and bags, watching Stephen defiantly all the while.

"Your weapons—"

"I will keep my father's sword!" George cut off Stephen. He took his sword from Joanna and buckled the scabbard at his waist. "My seconds will keep what weapons they have!" he added. Turning, George signaled the rest of his men to retreat and once Richildis was out of the carriage, he dismounted and bade his sister and Joanna follow suit.

They walked single file up a hillock towards the walls of Eskeleth. George made ready to stop at the gatehouse but saw that it would have been useless— the guards were standing at attention, but their eyes were dull and they were lifeless, as if they had drank from the same cup as their lady Richildis. It was the same as they walked through the streets. The only sound was the scuff of the shoes and mailed boots on the cobblestones, the creaking of harness.

"Joanna!" Petronelle whispered, coming up and taking her hand.

"What is it?"

"Look around you!"

Having kept her eyes downcast during their trek, Joanna now glanced about and frowned.

Everything was gray, or blue-gray, or black-gray, or just gray, perhaps white. Even the people of Eskeleth looked drained of color. Joanna knew on overcast days, everything seemed colorless except foliage, but here, everything was made up of the same hues, and everything was bleak. She glanced down at her hands and was relieved that there was color in them—she was glad that her days of poverty had made them tan and look healthy. Looking at her sleeves, she was glad the woolen gown was still the same rose color and her surcote a dark green. She turned and saw that the rest of their party looked normal, but they were as perplexed as she was at what lay around them.

"Ah! My lord Wulfstan's chancellor, Osprey FitzWalter, has arrived before us; I see his standard below that of Wulfstan's," Stephen announced happily when they passed through the gate house. "There! He waits for us."

Posturing on the top of the stairs to the donjon was the specter from George's childhood. Finally he could put a name to that demon. Today, however, Osprey looked more like a crane than a crow or bird of prey with his gangly body lost in brocaded velvet that made his frame smaller and insignificant. The wisp of a beard and mustache were as sharp and pointed as his face, which may have been handsome in youth.

Osprey made no effort to come forward as the party came through the narrow foregate. Courtiers and ladies, as drab and lifeless as the townspeople, moved slowly out of their way.

"My lady," Osprey greeted Richildis when she climbed the steps. His obeisance was like a reed bending in the wind.

"You kept your promise, Osprey," Richildis said tartly as the man lingered over her hand much too long for her liking. "And so have we. We bring George Ascalon, earl of Grasmere, to pay the blood debt owed to Eskeleth."

"What debt?" George and Petronelle asked at once.

The answer came later while they sat with Wulfstan in his solar. Seated on fur-draped benches, Petronelle and George were given places of honor among the household retainers, who George wanted to poke or prod to see if they were even alive, so quietly and still they sat or stood. The arrival of a young girl with a harp startled him, for she threw back the door from an anteroom and dragged a harp.

With little ceremony she plopped down on a cushion and began to play.

"A blood debt is nothing foreign to you, my lord," Wulfstan answered; his nasal, high-pitched voice grating against the more unpleasant and monotonous three-note tune the girl offered.

"There has been no enmity between our families so far as I know," George protested. "Why should there be such a price? And for what purpose?"

"I forgave Grasmere's betrayal and deceit and required that for our turning a blind eye, your father or his eldest son would come at my bidding whenever asked and do whatever asked on pain of death."

"No!" Petronelle exclaimed.

"Sister…" George cautioned, and then asked, "What does Eskeleth require?"

"To destroy an evil that has taken us."

"How shall I do that? Your daughter says your land has been in this wasted state for a generation."

"You will do what is required."

"And in exchange for my service, Eskeleth will give me a thousand crowns and one-half of its estates and swear fealty to the earls of Grasmere."

"If you survive," Wulfstan replied, a smile crossing his lips.

"It shall not be borne!" Petronelle cried. "My brother is no longer a Crusader and will not risk his life and limb for something that was never his fault!"

"Silence!" Wulfstan shouted. "Lady, your opinion is not required at this council."

"What concerns me is the concern of my sister. She has every right to oppose this crusade, for what will become of her if something should happen to me? Will you escort her back to Cumbria into the hands of our mother?" George said quietly. He looked from Wulfstan, to Richildis, to Stephen and then Osprey, waiting. As expected, they did not respond. "I didn't think so."

"I will not be given away like a concubine, nor sold to one of your gray lords!" Petronelle hissed.

"Be silent, girl!" Richildis growled. To George she smiled and purred, "You must be sure to succeed, my lord. You've fought against worse evil than ours. This should be nothing to you."

"I've heard much of this evil, lady, but it has not been described, nor explained, nor revealed. A dying man has a right to look his executioner in the face."

Wulfstan nodded, rising from his chair of state and went to a southern window where the distant spires and towers of the city of York stood out like pin pricks against the sky and the marches and moors of the shire were rich stripes of brown, gray and green. Pulling back the heavy shutters allowed a sickly yellow light to pour into the room as if the sun was setting behind a veil of mallow. More steam drifted in and with it a stench of sulfur and roasting meat. He motioned George to the window.

"Do you see that hill in the distance? Set in the ruined coppice?" Wulfstan asked.

George squinted in the light, looking where he pointed. The coppice was evident; it looked like a faery ring, a macabre circle of dancers that had been frozen for all time. George saw nothing set in the coppice except the charred remains of what used to be a farm, and, of all things, a tree that still lived and was as green and bountiful as in midsummer.

"I see a coppice, but naught else—and a tree," George answered honestly.

"Tell me again that you do not see it!" Wulfstan hissed, stretching his hand and arm farther out the window.

"I tell you, sir, I see nothing but dead trees, what's left of a farm, and a tree, though how it stands untouched—"

"That is our devil. It takes different forms—to each opponent it comes in different guises."

"What, the tree?" George and Petronelle cried in unison.

"The creature that sleeps nearby!" Wulfstan hissed.

"I see nothing, Wulfstan, but I suppose you'll call it a wyvern or dragon or the devil if it contents you!"

"Why do you mock us? It sleeps now, but in a month, it will wake and demand payment. The countryside is scarred from battles lost trying to vanquish it. Our herds are decimated for it devours our sheep and our cattle. Worse still, we have been forced to sacrifice our people in every generation so that we may live for a time without fear."

"I think you do live in fear, Wulfstan!" George scoffed. "If I must fight, I will fight men, not the imagination."

Turning away, George was pulled back so that he was an eyelash away from Wulfstan's shriveled, gray, face. The man's eyes blazed and seemed to glow. George tried to free himself tactfully.

"Twenty-one years ago, the daughter of my chancellor was chosen by the Council to save Eskeleth. Her lover protested and offered himself in her stead. When the Council would have none of it, the fool stole her away to his lands. In doing so, he broke a contract of marriage between our houses—so not only did he put Eskeleth in mortal danger, but he also disgraced our families. He spurned my sister for this other woman. To prevent a war, an accord was made. In exchange for their life and safety, these lovers would, if God blessed them with sons, send the eldest boy to pay the debt. Or if there were no sons, he would return himself and honor his promise. The accord was signed in a blood pact."

Wulfstan raised his right hand and George saw the faint stripe of an ancient scar on the palm of his hand. "Now you know why your father insisted that you go on crusade. Death at the hands of the infidels would be better than what he sold you for!"

George moved away, trembling. Petronelle joined him, whispering, "It's all a fantasy, George! None of it can be true. Father is a better man than this fool Wulfstan makes him out to be!"

"If that were so, I would never have seen the scar on Father's hand!" George replied.

"Surely a battle wound, no more?" Petronelle offered.

"Why this secret counsel?" Wulfstan spoke out. "What needs must be done is decided."

"To ask that I—as my sister said, it is not to be borne!" George argued.

"It was your father who made this come to pass," Richildis spoke up.

"Your opinion is not wanted at this council!" George hissed.

"I give you until the morning to make up your

mind, my lord of Grasmere," Wulfstan said. "And then if you will not honor the promise to which you are bound, the lady Petronelle will take your place. A promise is a promise. Osprey will show you to your chambers. Come to me at sunrise with your answer."

✠✠✠

JOANNA PUSHED THE needle through the linen and tugged at the bright silk thread, bringing it up and over until the petal of a rose was completed. Twice she stuck her finger, but paid no mind; what bothered her more was the angry shouting coming from Petronelle's rooms. Roger and George screamed at one another, tossing accusations back and forth, and then Petronelle added her voice to the cacophony. This continued for hours. What amazed Joanna was how no one in the castle seemed to care. And there was the music. Somewhere in the castle a disturbing, three-note tune was plucked on a harp and the music irritated Joanna so that she threw her hands to ears and rocked back and forth.

"Please, please, God, make it stop!" she prayed.

"Roger!"

Petronelle's cry was followed by the slam of a door and footsteps down the winding staircase. Peering out the door, she saw George standing at the top of the stairs. When Petronelle flew out of the room George tried to hold her back.

"Idiot! Let go of me!" she growled and hurried after Roger.

As George turned to go back inside, Joanna ducked out of view and then closed the door quietly. Below, she heard the soft scud and clip of footsteps picking up speed. A glance out the window confirmed

Joanna's suspicions—Roger and Petronelle were taking flight; they wanted no part of this quarrel. Heartbroken, Joanna curled up on the bed and cried herself to sleep.

She woke hours later just as the watch sounded day's end. A deep, long note came from a horn somewhere in the castle. Her heart started to pound when she glanced around at the unfamiliar surroundings –the fine linen bed curtains and the silk and wool coverlets. She inhaled the stench and the steam and remembered they had arrived in Yorkshire and Lord Wulfstan had given them fine apartments in the round tower of the castle. Slipping between the bed curtains, she found her cloak and hurried out, going down into the courtyard in search of Adam. She hoped the boy would have an explanation for the quarreling, though none was truly needed. More than anything she wanted reassurance that she had not been left alone in Eskeleth.

Once out of the stairwell, Joanna glanced about for someone who might tell her where to find Adam. A maid was sweeping the spotless flagstones. She moved slowly and purposefully, over and over, oblivious to the girl standing in her path. The maid simply went around Joanna.

"I wonder if you could tell me where lord Middleton of Gawthorp is lodged." Joanna queried sweetly.

The broom moved back and forth, the straws scraping against the stones.

"You are not permitted, lady."

"He is a guest, as am I," Joanna said.

"You are not permitted, lady."

"If you would only point me in the direction of his chamber; or if you would send a message to him?"

"It would not be seemly. They will take my supper."

"But they will not. I will see that they do not." Joanna pulled the drawstring on the scrip dangling from her girdle and took out a coin, holding it out.

The maid pushed the broom towards Joanna's shoes, then a bit further, then stopped. The broom was pointing in the direction of the donjon.

"You've said well," Joanna whispered and pressed the coin into the maid's hand.

"The daughter of Merioneth will see much sorrow," the maid commented as Joanna hurried away. Hearing this, Joanna spun about to demand what she meant and saw that the maid was gone as if she'd never been. A broom lay on the flagstones.

The uncomfortable interview was forgotten and Joanna was still searching for Adam when she saw Petronelle and Roger walking through the gate house. They strolled at a labored pace, their faces as gray as their surroundings. The apparent anger displayed earlier had been replaced with dismay and resignation. Neither saw Joanna waiting for them in the tower stairwell until Roger pulled Petronelle into his arms and gave her a passionate, telling kiss. It was then Joanna's foot kicked a pebble on the stair and it rolled down to the couple locked in an embrace. Joanna looked away in embarrassment when they noticed her.

"Pray, little warrior, what do you see?" Roger asked softly, taking Joanna by the arm.

"Nothing, sir, but two turtledoves."

"And should the turtledoves fly away?"

"They would not, for our lord of Grasmere comes this way."

George appeared dressed in armor. "This is good, to find you together," he greeted. "I'm going to discover for myself what manner of devil it is that frightens people to death." He studied each in turn. "You're invited to come with me if you wish."

"I'm with you, sir," Joanna replied.

George looked at Petronelle and Roger, his large blue eyes assessing their guilty faces perceptively. "So you've decided to stay?" He asked.

"For the time being," Roger admitted, standing straighter and placing a hand on Petronelle's shoulder.

"We could not do otherwise, Brother," Petronelle whispered tearfully.

"I will understand if you do wish to leave, and give you my blessing," George said in passing.

"George," Roger started, hands spread wide in supplication, but George dismissed the gesture with a shake of his bowed head as he walked on.

✠✠✠

NO ONE SEEMED to care that four people left the safety of the castle and headed for the coppice beyond the city walls. The townspeople went about as if nothing was amiss and that life draped in a perpetual shroud was normal. Roger did his best to attract attention, talking loudly to George and scraping his sword on the cobblestones, but people scarcely noted this as they moved slowly going to and fro on whatever business compelled them out of doors.

Outside the walls, the stench of death and decay

was so overwhelming that Joanna felt ill and knelt by the side of the road and heaved.

"You should go back," George murmured as he helped her to her feet.

"I must go forward with you," she gasped and looked up at him with a weak, sincere, smile. "You do understand?"

George nodded and brushed the back of his hand lightly against her cheek.

As they walked south to another cropping of hills and around to the coppice, George sensed that they were being watched, though there was not a living thing between castle and coppice save his party.

The path was strewn with charred branches and smoldering rocks, with the rotting carcasses of animals and men. The ground was black and glistening as if made of onyx. If trees stood along the path, they were stripped of all life and nothing more than blackened trunks with skeletal branches that reached out like tentacles.

Finally, the coppice.

It was a ring of what used to be ancient oak trees standing in the middle of nowhere. A half-league distant was the lone tree, an ancient apple tree that seemed as large as the coppice. The fruit was red and ripe, inviting. George drew his sword from its sheath as he walked cautiously into the ring. As he approached, he sensed movement to his left and wheeled about, expecting to find a demon and seeing only the smoldering remains of a bush.

"There's nothing here," Roger said behind him; "the old man is sick with fantasies."

George was about to agree when he saw

something move out of the corner of his eye and turned slowly. "Impossible!" he whispered. Standing before him were eight men with swords ready; men he led to their deaths in Constantinople.

CHAPTER 12

*I*MPOSSIBLE! GEORGE THOUGHT as he stared at the men. He took a cautious step forward, gripping the sword with two hands. None of them moved; in fact, as George looked carefully, they all held the stare of dead eyes, yet he could see their chests rising and falling with slow, easy breath.

"I saw you die at Constantinople!" George cried.

"George?" Roger was with him now. "George, what is it?"

"This cannot be!"

"What? A few rocks, some burnt trees, charcoal."

The eight men started to walk forward, slowly at first, and it seemed as though they were coming from a great distance. Suddenly they picked up speed and raised their swords, filling the air with the shrieks and moans George remembered from the Forest of Kentmere. George let out a yell and began cleaving with his sword until it was soaked in blood and not a man was left standing.

And then he saw something—the figures were blurred as if they were moving rapidly, but it was unmistakable as to what was happening.

"No!"

"George! George, what madness has taken you?"

He dropped his sword at the sound of Roger's voice and started to weep, his shoulders sagging, his strength gone. When he looked up, Roger and Joanna were kneeling beside him, Petronelle standing a safe distance away; she too was weeping. George reached for his sword and saw how it sparkled in the pale light, as clean and sharp as the day it was forged. He looked at his armor and gauntlets—they were just as clean. The coppice was empty. Feeble breezes made a dried leaf skip over the ground and stir up the black and gray dust.

As soon as George was on his feet, he sprinted back to Eskeleth, the others in his wake, calling for calm and trying to catch up. Once George burst into the great hall, he found his quarry and made straight for Osprey, grabbing him by the neck and throwing him up against a wall.

"What game is this?" George screamed as Osprey struggled to break free. "Is that how you do it, old man? Play with the mind and heart?"

"George! Let go of him! You're killing him!" Petronelle shouted as she ran into the great hall ahead of Joanna and Roger. Roger managed to pry the two men apart and shoved George into a chair. Osprey didn't move save for arranging his collar and chain of office. After a moment, though, he smiled at George and left the chamber.

"Look at you!" George now shouted at the courtiers standing idly in the hall. "You're all ghosts! You're as dead as this godforsaken place!"

"George," Petronelle murmured kneeling beside his chair. "Let's return to Skelwith. Father will understand."

"It's not Father's opinion I worry about!" he hissed.

"No one would fault you or your good name."

"I could change my name in an instant, but my soul?"

The comment made Petronelle shy away and she rose quietly and stood beside Roger, touching his arm to get his attention. He smiled when she looked up at him imploringly and took him to one side. "What do you say, Roger? If there is anyone to help him see reason, to see the futility of this ridiculous quest, it's you. God forgive me, a miserable sinner, for ever wanting to come, for making him do this!"

"No," Roger said. "I think the sooner George rids Eskeleth of its curse, the better for all of us. And then we can go home."

***

Lord Wulfstan waved his secretary out of the solar when George was announced. Without a word, he offered a cup of ale, which was refused. George made ready to speak when he noticed Richildis seated on the cushions by the window. "I will speak to you alone," he growled at Wulfstan.

"My daughter is my second and equal in all things, Lord Grasmere; you will learn this when you marry her."

George shot an angry look at Richildis, who was paying more attention to her needlework than wonted. "And in what fantasy might that be?" he demanded.

"When you have vanquished our enemy."

"It was never a condition of my service to you!"

"But it is, and I expect you to honor it. Your father refused to marry my sister. I don't think you'd be so imprudent as to deny her niece, my daughter, who excels my late sister in beauty and virtue."

"How will that change anything?" George demanded.

"Must I explain honor to you, a knight?"

"No, my lord, it is you who must explain to me what this masque is!"

"So you think our misfortune is a masque. Likewise, you think it a pastime, or entertainment!" Wulfstan scoffed.

"For yourselves, perhaps. You prey on weakness, on memories!"

"Do I? I would I knew what you were talking about."

George nearly pounced on him, taking Wulfstan by the collar and held him close so that he could barely breathe. "You open a man's wounds; you play with foul memories and misfortunes."

"Enough!" Richildis ordered as she came between them. George released Wulfstan only because he was startled by her action and liveliness. "Father, George will undertake to honor the Grasmere pledge," Richildis continued, but her words were cut off by the slamming of the great doors as George left. Joanna came in unannounced soon after and after a slight obeisance to Wulfstan, turned on Richildis.

"What are you about, lady?" Joanna hissed. "Why do you not see or understand the torment—"

"He is in a foul state, mistress. Perhaps you can talk sense to him. George hangs on to your words like they were Holy Scripture," Richildis purred.

"For myself and not for you!" Joanna said on her way out.

The clang and timbre of swords, mace, and morning star told Joanna that George was in the tiltyard. He was with Adam and Roger and all three were dressed for combat.

"Again!" George growled at Roger.

"I'm done for now. A sovereign on Adam," Roger jested, handing over his shield and sword to the wide-eyed boy waiting his turn.

Once Adam was armed and ready, Roger gave the signal. George was taken off guard by the boy's swift and powerful attack and tried to keep up with him, missing the mark and his footing time and again. He could see Adam's large brown eyes glinting from behind the visor and heard Roger's laughter over his labored breaths resonating in the helmet. At the edge of his line of sight he noticed Joanna and in that brief second, Adam knocked him off guard and threw him to the ground.

"Will my lord yield?" Adam laughed.

"Again!" George panted, scrambling to his feet.

"If ever a man was ready for this contest, my lord, it's you," Roger said. "Let's begin again tomorrow and call it a good day's work."

"Again, damn you!"

"Really, sir, I don't think—" Adam began.

"Would you accept my challenge?" Joanna called out.

George removed his helmet, unsure of what he'd just heard. She approached, sword in hand. He shook his head and lowered himself on to a bench, stripping off armor. Joanna pitched the sword into the hard earth and the men stared in wonder as the blade was driven deep, swayed back and forth.

"Lady Richildis sent me to talk sense to you, my lord, but I would rather reason with you in familiar terms," Joanna said. "So, would you accept my challenge?"

"Joanna!" George groaned.

"It is because I'm a woman, or because you're weary?" she asked, bemused.

"Neither," George answered, taking a long drink from the wineskin Roger offered.

"Because I am a woman, you think I am weak, frail, and timid."

"No. You proved yourself admirably in Kentmere Forest."

Adam jerked his head at Roger and they retreated quietly, having no desire to be a part of a quarrel they knew George wouldn't win.

"Just so. Let me prove myself again in familiar terms."

"It isn't that," George said, not daring to look at her. She stood over him now, blocking out the pale sun.

"It could be nothing else, I think!"

A breeze whipped tendrils of her hair about, brought color into her cheeks. He wanted to say something bawdy, to suggest she was made for gentler sport, terms they'd both negotiate in bed, but he couldn't—it would offend her even more; he was sure of that.

George finally looked up, meeting her gaze. "Do you want to know what I saw in the coppice?" he asked quietly.

"What did you see?" It came as a tentative whisper, not a request.

"I saw my death—and yours."

George pushed himself off the bench and walked towards the donjon. For the remainder of the day he locked himself in his chamber, coming out only to dine with his sister and companions. Even the offer of Joanna's company could not dissuade him from a self-imposed confinement. He was gone as soon as supper was done, leaving the others without a single courtesy. And so it happened on the nights and days that followed. As soon as George was gone, Roger and Petronelle quarreled quietly while Adam and Joanna kept a secret counsel, choosing to play chess or dice, or read passages of scripture aloud from a Bible they found hidden in a cupboard.

No one spoke of what was truly on their minds, or expressed their fears.

Adam studied the chessboard between them and smiled, moving his king a square.

"If you make that move, sir, I shall have you in checkmate," Joanna purred. She slid her queen in a diagonal and picked up Adam's king, saying, "Checkmate!"

"I remember the last game," Petronelle spoke up. "George demanded a kiss."

Adam looked to Petronelle and Roger for approval and when they nodded, glanced at Joanna nervously. Smiling, Joanna let him buss her gently on the lips and the boy flushed with bright color. "I take such liberty and pleasure on behalf of our good lord of Grasmere," he pronounced.

Joanna touched his cheek in a sisterly fashion and

went to the window that faced the great tower.
Looking out as she had on so many evenings in the
last month, she found George sitting at the desk,
writing. What did he write she wondered, on this, the
last night before battle?

✠✠✠

NOT SINCE THE age of six when he had fallen from
his father's horse had George wanted a nursemaid's
comforting arms. Tonight he found his comfort in a
flask of wine taken from the feast Wulfstan held in his
honor. He decided to spend his last hours on earth
listening to the strange, if disturbing, music that
wound through the castle corridors and chambers
from the great hall, taking account of his short life's
accomplishments—and getting drunk.

Seated by a window that faced the coppice and
the round tower where Joanna and Petronelle lodged,
George took sips of wine between writing items on a
page. When he had written a list, he held it up to the
candlelight and nodded.

Nothing on the list would have merited praise
from anyone. Two of his accomplishments stood out:
that he had survived the sack of Constantinople and
he succeeded his father in the earldom of Grasmere.
Few of his friends could say the same. Truth be told,
he had few friends. Next, there were the list of
friends—very few on that list. Following this, a list of
the women he had loved, or thought he had loved.
This list was longer than the rest, and his eyes
continually fell to one name: Aurelia.

Smiling, George remembered her sweet face as he
rode out of Constantinople, remembered how
exciting their lovemaking had been, how he ached for

her on the long journey home—and how she had betrayed him.

George struck her name from the list.

The pen hovered over the parchment momentarily, and George began the letter 'J' and just as suddenly scratched it off, and then made hatch marks through his many lists, his many accomplishments in a life that seemed to disappoint everyone, even himself.

The true accomplishment would be surviving his battle with Wulfstan's fertile imagination.

The hourglass marked three hours until dawn. George tapped on the glass and a clump of sand dropped ominously into the bowl. He watched the grains slide through the narrow channel until he was bored and looked about for something else to amuse him. What George thought was curious was the absence of conversation or laughter in the great chamber below. All that stuffed his ears was the dismal, strange music.

George turned to study the pile of books on the shelf behind him and while he sorted through histories and philosophies he felt the sting of an insect on the back of his head, and then another. George slapped away the bugs until he realized someone was shooting pebbles at him from the round tower. He looked out the window and saw Joanna making ready to fire again.

"If you poke out an eye, I'll not be able to attack Wulfstan's imaginary demons!" George called. "What mischief are you up to?"

"There's a garden on the roof of the donjon," Joanna called, pointing above George's head. "Shall I tell you there?"

George craned his neck out the window and stretched even further to see where she pointed, perilously close to tumbling out to a certain death. "There's nothing up there."

"I can see it as plainly as I can see you. You're in your cups again, aren't you?"

"I'll meet you and then we'll see who's right and who's wrong. Shall we make a wager?"

"Ah, no! For I know what you have in mind!"

Smiling for the first time in days, George picked up the candle and his cloak on the way out. He found the wooden bridge that led to the donjon and a stairway opening out into a passageway that ultimately brought him into a walled garden just as Joanna noted—and on the roof of the donjon, of all places.

His breath caught at the sight before him. Herbs and flowering plants were carefully laid out in patches of bright color among fruit trees and shade trees. A cobbled path wound through flower beds and small hedges, and along the four walls that kept this Eden secluded were sedilia carved of the finest marble, as if this were a chapter house and contemplatives came here to chant the hours. Cresset lamps swung from poles and made it possible to come here at night, for one false step and it was a plunge of at least a hundred feet to the ground.

George was struck by the scent of perfume. Everywhere in the castle held a stench of decay and burning flesh, but here the air was not so tainted— and the color! Where the walls and the people seemed drained of life, this garden offered bright, hot, color that charged all the senses.

When the light footsteps on the casement announced Joanna's arrival, George spun around and nodded in greeting, feeling the color rise in his face and his breath quicken just being with her.

"This truly is amazing," George said, glancing about. "It's Eden."

"I'd like to think it's the only place evil hasn't touched—or cannot." Joanna took a step forward. "How are you?"

"All things considered, well enough."

"Your sister sleeps soundly—she doesn't know I'm gone."

"Or she's waiting to tiptoe into Roger's chambers, or he into hers."

They laughed nervously and George shoved his hands into his belt and puffed out a sigh, wondering what to say next, and hoping he would not say anything foolish.

"I wanted to wish you good luck; you've kept apart from us," Joanna started.

"The result of guilt; a great fear of what should become of all of you if I fail. My dreams have been of what will befall you. I see you all becoming ashen, gray, silent, lifeless, like everyone here, and—"

"Enough! Enough, sir! The fault lies with your father."

"I shouldn't have brought you and my sister, nor put you in such danger," he admitted.

"But that's the whole point, isn't it? To face the unknown and prevail against it? Do you think Lady Richildis would have told you the truth?"

George laughed softly. "That sounds like jealousy to me; something I'd not expect from you."

"I suppose when you've vanquished whatever beast lies in wait, Lord Wulfstan will expect you to marry his daughter; I mean to say—well, I've read the ancient legends and there it is."

"It was mentioned."

"Ah! Well, it stands to reason."

"Would you care?"

"It's not my place to worry about such things, my lord."

George approached slowly, saying, "Yet you have come to fare me well, and she has not."

They were in the shadows of apple trees that threw branches out from the trunks like canopies. When George stood before her, Joanna's face was obscured by the darkness. He tentatively reached out to touch her cheek and was surprised by the dampness of a tear as it slid down his thumb. "You are a puzzle to me!" he whispered.

"I am afraid for you! You saved me from death, yet I cannot save you!"

"Pray for me?" George murmured and lifted her chin for a kiss.

Joanna put her arms around his neck and pressed against him as their kisses became deeper and ardent and it wasn't until a raven cawed and startled them that Joanna broke away and whispered, "I will pray for you, George!"

"Wait!" George called, catching her before she disappeared down the stairs. A moment passed before he said, "It's my custom to spend a night in prayer before a battle. Stay with me."

"It would be said—"

"—that you kept vigil in a church."

They went down the stairs and at the landing he stopped and smiled up at her. "You called me George," he said softly, offering a kiss.

"So I did."

An hour searching the donjon and buildings crowded within the baileys revealed bakeries, butteries, dovecotes, smiths, herb sheds, but no chapel. Ready to concede defeat in their quest, George caught the ruby glow in a window of one of the smallest buildings beside the southwestern gate.

"A sanctuary lamp!" he murmured and led the way.

It was a chapel long in disuse. The door was stiff and frozen with age, but after several tries, it creaked open, the dry, ancient door splintering as the latch gave way in George's hand.

The musk of decades of candle wax and flowers, mildew and earth filled their lungs with a pungent cloud.

Where dust and cobwebs hadn't touched the furnishings, moss covered them. Even the fair linen on the stone altar where a paten, chalice, and purificator were laid out, waiting for the celebrant, was enclosed in a shroud of webs.

Joanna turned the pages of the Bible, sure that they would crumble in her hands, but gasped when she found the holy book as fresh and new as if the pages had been illuminated only that morning. She heard George's soft exclamation and looked where he did—the sanctuary lamp light had grown brighter. There had to be an explanation; perhaps the fresh air that streamed in from the courtyard. Still, they watched the flame sputter and grow. Silently, Joanna

followed George to the rail before the sanctuary and
knelt beside him, her movements stirring up ancient
dust. There they kept vigil until the sky began to turn.
When they slipped away, they didn't see the single
flower, a lily, which had sprung to life on the credence
shelf beside the ambry.

CHAPTER 13

THE ROAD FROM castle to town was scattered with a sparse showing of people who rose early to watch their newest champion do battle. Standing at a window of his bedchamber, George looked down at the people as still and gray as the landscape. He felt movement to his right and smiled at Petronelle.

"You go to your death and they show only indifference," she murmured, slipping her arm through his.

"Are you so certain I won't succeed?" George scoffed.

"George! Forgive me; I am so used to hearing our lady mother's barbs and criticisms. Of course you will prevail!"

"If only to prove her wrong." George leaned down to kiss her forehead. "But your prayers will not be unwelcomed, Little Pet!"

Petronelle gasped and smiled up at him through tears. "It's been so long since you called me that!"

"When I return we'll see about mending old wounds."

A knock on the door, then, and Roger and Adam appeared with Wulfstan. Both were armed in expensive harness and Wulfstan wore cloth woven of gold thread and embellished with golden beads and buttons, with crystals and ribbons so that he was the only living thing in Eskeleth that had color, save the champion George and his party.

"It's time," Roger said, coming forward.

"Joanna's not with you?" George asked, looking around him.

"Lord of Grasmere, see what we have given you," Wulfstan interrupted and pointed out the window. Looking down, George was surprised to find a spirited stallion, richly caparisoned in the Grasmere colors and wearing his saddle. The horse was pure white and resembled his favorite, Leofwine, the horse killed under him in Constantinople. Grooms were bringing forward two more horses for Roger and Adam, who both exclaimed at their beauty. George knew better than to ask how this came about and stood silently while Roger armed him.

"Where is she?" George whispered when Roger handed him the sword of Ascalon.

✠✠✠

NO ONE IN the crowd moved or spoke as George rode out with Roger and Adam. The irritating, if not painful three-note tune was replaced by the sound of a breeze that made the hems of skirts and cloaks flicker and veils dance. It sounded like the howling of wounded animal, and worse, it reeked of sulfur. Only when George approached the outer curtain of the Golden Tower did the air seem to clear and the noise stop. There was Joanna standing on the steps of the chapel with Petronelle. He paused at the steps and raised the visor to his helmet so that they could see his smile. As one they knelt and bowed their heads. George lowered his lance in tribute and after a long, last look, slammed the visor down again and kicked his spurs into the horse's flanks, picking up speed as he rode off. By the time he reached the coppice, Roger and Adam were at pains to keep up with him.

The ring had been transformed since his last visit. A pavilion had been raised across from the apple tree. A single cot with blankets, a chest, a table, a bench, and carpets were the only furnishings, but they were exquisitely wrought and appointed pieces.

"Do they think this is a tournament?" Adam scoffed as he entered and looked around. "The last I saw a pavilion as fine as this was in London at the games for the duke of Cornwall."

"This is a more dangerous game," George murmured.

Roger frowned, hands on hips as he went to the cloth-draped table. "Not even a cup of wine! Well, had I a cup and wineskin, I would drink to my liege lord, the earl of Grasmere. May his siege be brief and his life long."

"To Grasmere and God!" Adam crowed.

"To God!" George whispered.

The stench of sulfur wafted into the tent and a dank mist started to dance around them. It was unbearably hot and then bone-chilling cold again. George moved his hand to the sword by his waist and watched the shadows on the tent canvas, expecting to see a monstrous silhouette. When it grew still, he put on his helmet and went out.

Osprey stood in the midst of the barren coppice, as twisted and bleak as the naked trees. He cackled, something akin to a laugh, and then bowed.

"Good morrow, young George."

"And you, sir."

"Succeed, and you will restore the honor of Ascalon. Fail—"

"Shall we begin?"

Osprey nodded and stepped back, rapping his staff upon the ground. As he continued in his retreat, the land quaked and more of the disgusting sulfuric mist rose from fissures, engulfing George. When the mist cleared, George felt as if he had awakened from a deep sleep, his eyes heavy and his thoughts confused. Glancing about, he spun round and saw that the pavilion and coppice were gone and he was alone on the precipice of a hill— and not just any hill, but Golgotha in Jerusalem. Gone was the church erected on the site where the Christ had been crucified. In its place stood a beautiful young knight, who was nothing less than perfection.

He was dressed all in white and the sun shone so brightly off his white silver armor that it was painful for George to look at him. His hair was glossy black and fell to his shoulders. The eyes looked to be the color of the brilliant sky above them. When he came forward to offer his courtesy, George saw great, white wings with the palest blue and pink edges, and as he came nearer, the light those wings gave off was brighter than any star or sun and nearly blinded him.

"Gesu! I'm to fight Saint Michael!" George whispered in horror.

"Come, sir! You are fit for three contests," the archangel said in a voice that was surprisingly low and melodious to George's ear. "Prove victorious, George Ascalon of Grasmere, and you will have favor. Surely there is no one on earth so righteous, even you, as to do good without ever sinning!"

George swallowed the lump in his throat and took a breath to control his trembling, speaking in a strong, even voice that belied his state of mind, he said, "Let the outcome be God's will."

"Well said!"

Suddenly George felt as if he had been lifted into the air and thrown down like a pebble or dried leaf in a windstorm. Amazed he was still alive, George looked around and saw three empty crosses towering above him, the blood of a crucifixion still fresh and wet, sliding down the wood of the cross standing in the middle. Whispering a prayer, George closed his eyes to banish the sight and saw the plunder of a monastery in Constantinople instead. A scream filled his ears; George was surprised to realize that it came from his throat. When he caught his breath, the archangel attacked again, but this time George was ready and threw a strong, murderous blow that knocked him, and not his opponent, on to his backside. Again, George felt lightheaded and dizzy, as if he were being spun about. Another prayer formed on his lips and George found his footing and swung again, hitting his quarry and throwing the archangel onto his knees. George attacked again and again, advancing rapidly with every strike and renewed vigor, and it seemed as though he would take this first contest.

The archangel began to laugh, though it sounded like the bellowing of a wounded animal and then changed to roars and hissing. The beautiful archangel was slowly changing before his eyes with every blow met, the white silver armor turning to bright, golden fur, the fine, almost feminine features becoming leonine, the wings made of gold and copper scales until the great form of St. Mark, the winged lion, stood before him. It rose up on hindquarters and roared, flames as bright and golden as the sun spewing from its mouth.

George gave a murderous shout as he found new strength and attacked. He was getting the best of the lion when the olive trees around them began to drip with blood. The air was choking with sulfur again and the lion coughed fire, shooting flames at George, who dodged and leaped to get out of the way. And then he felt as if he had been caught up in a whirlwind like those he'd experienced in the desert near the Jordan River, moving blindly as sand and dust made it impossible to see; the howl of the wind was deafening. The lion was charging now and inhaled until its breast swelled like a ship's main sail, the beating of its heart visible.

George closed his eyes and threw his sword like a spear, hearing a roar of pain as the weapon struck. He then screamed as flames and scalding vapors overwhelmed him. He was falling out of control, thrown from Golgotha, the landscape and buildings of Jerusalem colorless shapes and blurs as he careened, the lion spiraling downward after him so that George was in peril of colliding with it. The lion was flailing and struggling to gain control of its descent. The ground was only a league away now. George fell quickly, tumbling purposefully towards the lion so that he grabbed on to its great wings, and mounted it like a horse, riding the rest of the way down, hoping to break his fall when they landed, if he survived . . .

And then he opened his eyes and found himself lying on the ground in the coppice. Roger and Adam stood over him, swords ready. Roger threw down his sword and helped George to his feet.

"Did you see it, my lord?" Adam cried. "The fog came as if from nowhere and we couldn't see our hands before our faces!"

"Adam!" Roger snapped. "If you've strength to talk, you've strength to go back to the castle. Tell the lady Petronelle to come as quickly as she can. And if her royal self is in an excellent humor, bring the lady Richildis, too."

"Leave me!" George gasped. "Get away from here!"

"God's wounds, George, you look as if you've been fighting in the Holy Land," Roger said to George when they were alone. "Whatever it was, it happened too fast. I blinked my eyes and you were lying on the ground, writhing as if you were plagued by demons. Let's get you into the pavilion."

Throwing one of George's arms about his shoulders, Roger helped him to the pavilion and on to the bed and shouted at Adam to be quick about his business. The boy had no trouble pushing through the crowd of spectators for they parted before him like reeds in the wind and didn't bother to look back as he sped past them. Adam hadn't gone far when Petronelle and Joanna overtook him on the road from the castle.

"Is he dead?" Petronelle demanded, grabbing Adam by his shoulders.

"He lives, lady! He lives," Adam panted for

breath. "Lord Mowbray bade me come and fetch you." When Joanna made no move to go with them, he took her hand. "Why tarry, Mistress? He will surely want to see you."

Again the crowd parted as Adam came through but this time there were rumblings of disapproval when Petronelle and Joanna followed on his heels. Roger came from the pavilion and met them in the coppice.

"We heard trumpets," Petronelle said, catching her breath and leaning against Joanna for support.

"Trumpets? We heard no trumpets," Adam interjected.

"There were trumpets," Joanna insisted. "Lord Wulfstan assured us the contest was over for the day; the great knight—"

"What did you see?" Roger interrupted.

"I saw nothing, in truth," Adam scoffed.

"I swear upon my life I saw him!" cried Joanna. Looking at them in turn, she continued. "First there was George and you with Adam, and then suddenly a mist came over the hillock and we couldn't see a thing."

"Aye, there was a fog of sorts."

"When the mist cleared, there was a knight standing alone, but the sun caught his armor and blinded us. It couldn't have been my lord of Grasmere, for though he stands taller than most men, this knight was almost as tall as the tree—"

"You saw what? There was no knight!" Roger laughed.

"I tell you, sir, there was a knight—a great man, much taller than Grasmere, and he was so beautiful to look at until his armor caught the sun and I had to look away. Then he was gone and my lord Grasmere was nowhere to be found," Joanna insisted.

"Do you mean to say he fled?" Petronelle demanded.

"I do not mean to say that, my lady."

"Surely my brother fought honorably!"

"Come see for yourself and judge whether he fought honorably or not," Adam snapped.

Petronelle said nothing but entered the pavilion and went to the bed where George was sprawled, his arm over his face. She raised the arm gently and sighed in relief that he looked whole. As she moved away so that Joanna could see for herself, George took Petronelle's hand and tried to pull her closer. He cried out in pain and Joanna used the soft fabric of her long sleeve to wipe the sweat, dirt and blood from his face.

"Be easy, my lord!" Joanna whispered, gently washing him.

"I'm thirsty!" he gasped.

Joanna looked around and saw there were no ewers or flagons standing ready. She turned to Petronelle. "Find some clean water!"

Eager to do her bidding, Petronelle went out and returned just as quickly. "There's nothing, Joanna! I shall send to the castle."

"We'll all go," Roger spoke up.

"And bring fresh linens, a change of clothes, and some unguent and spirits," Joanna instructed.

When the others had gone, Joanna returned to the bed and wept quietly as she ministered as best she could to George's wounds.

"I thirst!" George cried. "Please!"

Joanna wiped her tears and went to see where Petronelle and Roger had gone with Adam. The sun had managed to burn through the clouds of fog and now was so bright, she had to shield her eyes. What caught her attention however was the apple tree. It was still in full bloom and green, its branches heavy with fruit. Below it, a spring bubbled from the ground. "Goose girl!" she cursed, looking back at Petronelle hurrying alongside Roger, and now despaired of her new predicament. There was water, but what to put it in?

She caught sight of a courtier holding a great chalice and ran to him. Joanna looked up at his lifeless eyes and smiled. "Please sir, may I have this cup?" she asked.

As expected, he did not move but stared straight ahead, though he whispered and that whisper was picked up by others in the crowd and soon repeated on the lips of many, an ancient prayer.

"*Dominus tecum, Dominus tecum,*"

Joanna gently pried the chalice from his grasp and emptied it of its foul-smelling brew and then filled it to the brim with water from the spring, careful not to spill a single drop as she hurried back to George.

"Here, drink!" She implored.

George gulped the water, taking his fill. As he lay back on the pillows, Joanna cried out in surprise.

The wounds had healed on his face and hands and he looked as if he just taken a full night's rest. He smiled and asked, "I don't suppose there's anything to eat?"

Of course there was! Joanna ran and plucked some apples from the tree and fed them to George until he was sated and fell to sleep using Joanna's soft wool mantle for a blanket.

"My God!" Petronelle stood at the entrance with her arms full of linens and clothing, Roger and Adam behind her. "What sorcery is this? He looks whole!"

"There's a spring near the tree; he drank of the water. And apples. I gave him an apple." Joanna murmured, tucking the mantle around his shoulders.

"There's no such water," Petronelle argued.

"Aye, Joanna, I saw nothing outside," Roger said when he joined them.

"I tell you there's a spring!"

"Then it is in your imagination," countered Adam as he came in.

"See for yourself!"

Joanna led the way outside and pointed at the ground where the water bubbled and churned, a living spring, where the apple tree bowed under the weight of its fruit.

Roger frowned and shook his head. "You're weary, little warrior; you should come with us back to the castle."

"I shall stay. You go, if you like!"

"Roger speaks true, Joanna. You're as weary as my brother," Petronelle coaxed.

"I said I will stay!"

Joanna sat with George throughout the night. She dozed and nodded, waking with a start at his changes in breathing, or a gasp, a moan, even a snore. Towards dawn she shook sleep off and went out to find charcoal and wood for a fire. The tang of fresh air shocked her. And there was something else that jolted her to complete consciousness.

A songbird was offering measures as the sky brightened and the sun started to rise. Joanna cried out when she saw the coppice. Leaves were starting to sprout where dead wood used to be. To be sure she wasn't dreaming, Joanna plucked a blossom from one of the trees and inhaled its perfume. It was sweet and pungent. She ran into the tent and found George buckling on a sword.

"There's a difference this morning," he said in greeting. "It's hard to say what it is, but there is . . . something."

"Come and see," Joanna invited, reaching out for his hand. She led him out and they stood together marveling at the transformation.

"For this we should give thanks," George murmured. "Ride with me, Joanna."

George moved as easily and swiftly as he had the day before the contest. He led Joanna to his horse and helped her into the saddle, then swung up behind her, wheeling the horse about so that in moments they were headed for the castle. Joanna knew exactly where he was taking them—the little chapel.

The door gave way with little effort this time, and they could not help but notice the change. The flowers that had long lay as dry as parchment in their bowls were blooming with life and the sanctuary lamp glowed strongly and brightly. George knelt at the rails and bowed his head. For the longest time he stayed in prayer until he heard the horn sound. They rode at a breakneck pace back to the pavilion.

George expected to find Osprey waiting, perhaps a crowd of curious citizens, but dismissed the thought, knowing they wouldn't have noticed if the Archangel Michael flew down from heaven; they certainly didn't notice the morning before when he had done just that! George would enter this contest alone.

The coppice continued its transformation, its beauty startling and calming. George dismounted and helped Joanna down, walking into the coppice, hand on sword, waiting. The sound of birdsong made them look into the trees in wonder, as if hearing it for the first time.

Loud thunder and pounding chased the birds out of the trees. The earth trembled with every clap. Joanna grabbed George for support and she tucked the apple blossom between the gorget and breastplate of his armor. The morning light had dimmed and they looked up to see a giant man obscuring the sun's rays with his massive frame. He was handsome, with a neatly trimmed beard and dark, large eyes. On his forehead was a mark, as if he had been struck with something.

"Goliath," George whispered. To Joanna, he said, "Go inside and wait."

"God protect you!" she cried and kissed him. George watched her take shelter in the pavilion and then drew his sword, walking slowly towards his opponent, who smiled benignly, the corners of his eyes creasing and his eyes bright and blue.

"George of Grasmere! Are you so sure of yourself that you come without seconds?" the giant bellowed.

"No courtesy today, sir!" George answered and came at him. The giant blocked his attack with a force so amazing that George felt it through his entire body. Yet he did not falter, nor was he thrown about like chaff or seed as he expected.

And then the Goliath took a sling from his shoulder and placed in it in a shiny pebble so smooth and perfect that it seemed to be made of glass or molten gold and when it caught the sun George was blinded momentarily. He staggered back, and as soon as he was able to see again Goliath was winding the sling in circles above his head. When the stone was released there was a howling, a shriek so intense that George covered his ears, but the hideous sound could not be shut out. At the same time, clouds began to form in what once were bright skies. The stench of sulfur crept along with a fog, and everything started turning gray again.

Joanna watched through a slit in the tent canvas. The stone was hurling through the air towards George and it seemed to transform itself into a ball of fire as it drew closer. George held up his shield and blocked the attack. Goliath roared in frustration and launched another pebble, and that, too, turned into a comet of fire blocked by George's wooden shield. Now the pebbles were showered upon George, who managed to protect himself and was still able to attack and draw blood.

"Sweet Gesu!" Joanna whispered.

With every blow George managed, Goliath changed. The beard became scales and the scraggly hair turned into spikes. The dark eyes shrank into little crimson dots in a face that was pock-marked and

yellow, until finally a hideous ogre stood before
George, like that from the Little Langdale market.

The creature eased backwards and then arched in
a defensive stance.

George gripped his sword and shield until his
hands ached and waited, watching the clouds drift
past above him. As soon as the pale winter sun
revealed itself, George shifted the sword so that it
reflected a ray of light and blinded his opponent. The
creature was caught off guard and George attacked
again and again while it bellowed in agony, the shrieks
and moaning unbearable. George raised his sword
and swung it overhead; he felt as if he was being
swept into that horribly familiar whirlwind. When he
shook his head to clear vision and mind he found he
was on a street in Constantinople where knights
fought in hand-to-hand combat from house to house.
Women and children tried to run past them and were
cut down as houses burned and smoldered and the
cathedral bells tolled.

George let his sword fall on the creature and
found a crusader in its place. The man laughed and
threw a blow with a heavy broadsword already stained
with blood. He was surprised by the force of
George's return and reeled. George was gaining a
marked advantage when a young woman came from a
nearby courtyard. The lady moved slowly as if under
the influence of a strong potion; she paid no mind to
the warfare and butchery played out before her, but
continued to walk toward George.

George was ready to finish off the crusader when
he saw her face.

"Aurelia!" he screamed. His scream split the

skies and a torrent of steaming, hot, rain fell and thunderclaps rolled, as loud and frightening as trebuchet launches or the pounding of war horses on soft ground. Aurelia stopped an arm's length from George, impervious to the fighting around her and held out her arms to him, beckoning.

"You promised to return!" she called.

With one last, angry blow, George managed to end the Crusader's life. Just as the knight crumpled in a heap, Aurelia began to disappear; she blew away like dust, leaving an apple blossom.

He looked down and saw the apple blossom Joanna had given him. Picking it up, George realized that he had returned to the coppice. The air was sweet, and glancing at the trees, he saw that they bloomed ever more and the apple tree was still heavy with fruit. And then he was overcome by weariness. Every bone in his body ached, every sinew and hair was on edge. George leaned against the tree and slumped down. He closed his eyes and prayed for death.

CHAPTER 14

EORGE WOKE WITH the sun in his eyes. His head was cradled in Joanna's lap and she was bathing his face with a damp cloth. They were beside the spring and now Joanna put a cup to his lips. "Living water," she murmured, bidding him to drink. George gulped great mouthfuls of the water, his thirst unquenchable. "Are you hungry?" Joanna asked now and offered an apple. He took a bite and then gave the apple to Joanna and they shared it, passing the fruit back and forth, both listening to the music of the spring as it gushed and bubbled, the wind in the living trees.

George reached for Joanna. He gently brought her face to his and kissed her mouth. He was relieved when he opened his eyes to find her sweet smile and beautiful eyes, not the creature he feared, not Richildis.

They stayed under the apple tree until the light began to falter and dusk turned the sky purple, the sun an orange wash on the horizon. Joanna helped George to his feet and they entered the pavilion. Wordlessly, he lay down and beckoned to Joanna, who rested beside him and covered them with her mantle. They slept until dawn when the familiar, evil mist overtook the coppice and the ground was again jarred by pounding. As soon as George was armed,

Joanna took a needlework scarf from her pocket and tied it around his forearm. The great falcon and roses of Grasmere and the cross of Christ were entwined as one device and worked in perfect, luminous threads.

George came out of the tent and was surprised to find Petronelle, Roger, and Adam standing outside an enclosure made of a wooden frame and painted cloth that now surrounded the coppice.

Osprey came through the enclosure entrance and struck the ground with his staff and once again. The skies slowly turned to lead and the heavy clouds parted, allowing a great globe of fire to descend. At the same time, the mists grew brighter, their combined light shining off of George's armor and sword, until the spectators were forced to shield their eyes or go blind. When George was able to look again, he was facing Oswin FitzHugh, as real and alive as he had been the last time they met in Constantinople.

"Well met," Oswin greeted.

George nodded. "Have you come to take your measure of me," he asked, "or is this the end of our quarrel?"

"I never could duck, in a tiltyard or on a field. That's what you thought of me. Who was it that saved your life—and which one of us fled?"

Before George could answer for himself, Oswin attacked. This time, George was not thrown backwards or brought to his knees. He came at Oswin blow for blow and with boundless strength for each contest. George was ready to drive his sword in when Oswin's armor caught the sun and the reflected light blinded him. When he moved into the shade, it was

Aubrey facing him, though his father was younger and in full battle harness, his sword identical to the one George held.

"No!" George screamed.

"Come, boy, whose fault was it that brought you to this sorry state? Let me make amends," his father said.

It was Aubrey who attacked first, and George warded off the blow, pushing his father back with the flat side of his sword. The contest was more like a tiltyard exercise than a battle, for George remembered each of the stances, each of the blows as his father repeated them, offering praise with each assault.

"Consider your worth, George," Aubrey said; "no man could have done what you dared and survived— to countervail the orders of the doge of Venice and the kings of England and France, to help people escape, to fight your own men for the sake of Byzantines!"

"You sent me to die," George gasped.

"I sent you to atone for your life, such as it was!"

"I will not kill you!"

"Haven't you already?"

George paused, unsure of what Aubrey said, then rolled out of the way as his father swung the blade down. As they continued their fight, images flooded his mind's eye and plagued his memory. There was Marian, the merchant's wife of York, laughing as she bartered and bargained her husband's jewelry in their shop in The Shambles; George taking a first taste of her lips and love in her arms—and there was Aubrey with Marian in his bed; Maud's stricken face as George betrayed his father out of jealousy; there was

Elinor slipping into his bedchamber late at night, and then there was Aurelia . . .

Aurelia!

"I should have died the morning you returned from York. You have every right to take vengeance on me. Now come, my betrayals have ruined us. Finish me off!" Aubrey demanded.

"I said I will not!"

"Marian was her name. A merchant's wife from York. She wasn't enough; next came Elinor, and if I'd been in the Levant with you, I suppose I'd have taken the Byzantine girl—Aurelia, was it?" And there was another—"

George ran at his father. Aubrey tripped and fell, and again the sun was the arbiter. It caught on his gorget. George would have killed his father had the sunlight not blinded him. He staggered and fell. When he was able to see again, he was looking at a brass-scaled lizard with deadly talons and blood-red eyes, a menacing spiked tail.

The dragon, some called it. Some called it a wyvern.

It stood as high as a percheron, a great war horse, and was as long as George was tall, by twice the length.

"Adam! My horse," George ordered. Within moments, Adam brought a diffident stallion into the enclosure. It shied and balked, and the dragon spat an arrow of flame. Had George not mounted the horse and dug in his spurs, it would have been incinerated. George rode to the end of the enclosure as the flame found its mark on one of the trees, and then to the pavilion where Joanna waited, and took his shield from her.

"All shall be well," he whispered, and smiled.

Saying this, George dug in his spurs and the horse screamed, rising on its hindquarters, and then charged forward.

The dragon spat another flame, one that spanned the distance from the coppice to the Golden Tower. George threw up his shield, feeling the searing heat as he protected himself. At the same time, he attacked, and the dragon shied and then bellowed again. George threw blows without direction, letting them fall where they may. Twice he knew he'd done injury, for the dragon shrieked in pain and began to snap with its murderous, razor-like teeth. The horse was bitten in the neck and fell, George throwing himself out of the dragon's reach. His shield fell and rolled towards Joanna, who grabbed it as it fell into the spring. She managed to pull it out and made a short but perilous trek to give it to George, and then took cover behind the apple tree.

Arching its scaly, serpentine neck, the dragon coughed fire. George raised the shield and closed his eyes, waiting for the end. The dragon shrieked as if in pain and George looked over the edge of the shield to see that the fireball had returned and found its mark on the dragon's breast. George crept low and attacked, swinging with all his might at the beast. It felt as if he had struck a sack of grain or flour, for the sword lodged fast and would not be drawn. George pulled at the sword and used the shield to ward off the dragon's fiery blows as he struggled to dislodge his weapon.

Suddenly, the dragon howled and twisted about.

George took a quick glance and saw that Joanna was throwing apples at it! With the dragon so preoccupied, he was able to disengage the sword and with three great tugs, the sword all but flew out of the dragon's breast, the force throwing George up against the tree.

The dragon shrieked and howled and writhed in pain, blood coming in pulsing spurts from its wounds like macabre rain. It staggered and fell, then expelled a last breath. For the longest time, George sat on the ground, waiting, trying to catch his breath. Joanna stood above him, holding an apple in readiness, just in case. They hadn't moved by the time Adam, Roger, and Petronelle reached them.

Looking up and smiling wearily, George said, "Our work is finished here!"

✠✠✠

A NEW AND refreshing breeze passed through the coppice, bringing with it the scent of apple blossoms and rain though the skies were clear and the sun had never been brighter. Joanna stood at the entrance to the tent and watched as somber, silent workmen dismantled the spectator stands. George slept on the cot while his sister, Roger, and Adam sat in quiet conversation, making plans for their return to Cumbria and deciding what to do next, as if they had had any part in the horrible contests that had drained George of life and spirit. Ignoring Adam's invitation to join them and drink to George's victory, Joanna smiled and shook her head, walking out to the apple tree.

The hems of her skirts whispered against translucent fibers that were scattered over the ground, and when inspected more closely, looked to be scales that had fallen from the dragon growing cold and colorless at the far end of the pavilion. Joanna stooped to pick one up, curious, and held it to the sunlight. She saw soft shades of mauve, gray, blue, pink, and ivory, with specks of gold and silver reflected through the scale, much like the scale of a fish, but softer. As she rubbed it between her thumb and forefinger it became pliant, like woolen fiber. Soon it was a thick and thin thread, something to weave.

"The spoils of war."

Osprey's rasping voice startled Joanna and she crouched in place, ready to flee or pounce. He shuffled forward with the help of his staff and the uneven clip of his footfall and the tapping of the wood was almost mesmerizing. Joanna shook her head to clear her thoughts of the sound, knowing somehow that to pay attention would be to court death.

"'Tis but scales, like those of a snake or lizard," Joanna remarked.

"Many have come to champion us and all expected gold in payment, or titles and lands. They failed."

"George expects no less. Yet he prevailed. You cannot deny he is owed some payment."

"He knows what is right. And you. You have seen what the true prize is and you are knowing; you realize the gift you have," Osprey said quietly. He bent with some difficulty to meet her eyes. "Use it."

She took another scale between her thumb and forefinger, rolling the silky softness back and forth until a seemingly endless length of thread grew and breaking it with her finger, now rolled it into a ball. The thread itself glowed and felt warm, full of life. To hold the thread was holding security and protection. Joanna sat back on her knees and laughed.

"Of course!" she said to herself. "We're not done yet!"

And she gathered up as many scales as she could, using her surcote for a satchel.

"What's she doing?" Adam murmured, watching. Roger came to his side.

"Gathering blossoms?" he suggested.

"But nothing's there!"

"That's as may be, but we thought there were no apples, or stream," Roger commented, going back inside. He paused by the cot and held a hand over George's nostrils. "At least he lives."

"Of course he does!" Petronelle scoffed. "He could not have done otherwise! No lord of Grasmere would have failed."

"And yet your father..." Roger murmured and stopped when he noticed the angry set of Petronelle's brow and how she narrowed her eyes.

"Twice you consigned him to death, if I'm not mistaken," Adam spoke up.

"What business is it of yours? What part did you play? God's teeth, I suppose now that you and Roger will play out the contest in stories by mead hall fires as in olden times and bards will compose sagas naming you the heroes!" Petronelle hissed. "It is my brother who did this! It is my brother!"

Joanna purposefully tripping into the chest as she

returned silenced the argument. She merely glanced from one guilty face to another as he emptied her prizes on the lid of the chest and knelt to inspect them.

"What's all this, Joanna?" Petronelle wanted to know, coming to kneel beside her.

"They are George's spoils of the tournament. But see, it makes a wondrous thread." Joanna handed over one of several balls of thread she'd wound.

"Like jewels, but so soft and fine," Petronelle whispered as she held a scale and marveled how it became pliant, and then following Joanna's lead, spun it into a thread. Soon they were talking softly and looking every now and then at George, until hours later they had a dozen of the balls wound.

"What shall we do with it?" Petronelle wondered aloud.

"The old man said I should use it, but for what purpose I don't know," Joanna sighed and she glanced over at George who had turned in sleep for the first time in hours. "A victory banner!" she whispered.

"He will carry his deed into future battles!" Petronelle added. The shimmering thread reflected off Joanna's face and she held a ball to the girl's cheek. "It is meant for you, as well. See how the color brightens your face and eyes! Weave a cloth for yourself, Joanna."

"One that tells the valiant deeds of the lady of Merioneth."

George's comment brought the girls to his cot and they laughed and embraced him together. Roger and Adam joined them and soon they began to share

stories of George's three quests. While they talked
and laughed, Joanna listened. She sat apart from
them despite Adam's cajoling and wove the
luminescent threads into braids of yarn, sure she was
telling George's story – and hers.

CHAPTER 15

A s THE HOURS PASSED, the coppice flourished with new life and it seemed, Joanna remarked, that in all of Eskeleth there was thankfully another place filled with brightness. When Petronelle queried Joanna about this, Joanna blushed and said she must have dreamt the other. She avoided the puzzled glances from Roger, Adam and Petronelle and the smile George proffered. Her hope for a few hours more of happiness was dashed when Stephen arrived with an escort.

"You are fit to return to the Golden Tower, my lord?" Stephen asked after formal greetings were exchanged.

"I am more fit to return to Cumbria and my family, Master Langston," George replied and to prove that he rose unencumbered by fatigue or pain, motioned to Adam for his scabbard and sword. "Will you see that the preparations are made and that we may start our return journey on the morrow?"

"Lord Wulfstan would honor you first and for that reason I have come to bring you back."

"I have fulfilled my obligation."

Roger, Adam, Joanna and Petronelle had gathered round George and this defensive tactic was not lost on Stephen and his men. The Eskeleth guard placed hands on their swords, movements slow but deliberate and not lost on George.

"It would be unfortunate to slight Lord Wulfstan and the lady Richildis," Stephen said coolly. "They have waited many years for this celebration and nothing has been spared to honor their champion."

George and Stephen stared one another down. It was George who stepped away from confrontation and blinked first. Motioning to his companions, he said, "It will not be said that Aubrey of Grasmere's son is unthankful."

Bowing, Stephen replied, "We go first to the Tower where you each will find holiday robes fitting for our celebrations, and then we will go in procession to the great hall of Eskeleth where Lord Wulfstan and the Lady Richildis wait to do you honor.

✠✠✠

"THEY SHOULD BE cheering!" Petronelle whispered angrily.

Joanna nodded and looked out over the crowd towards the west entrance of the great hall where George had entered with Roger and Adam. The people of Eskeleth watched the procession with the same dull indifference as everything else in their lives. Despite the three men dressed in bright holiday clothes and especially George in golden armor and riding a pure white stallion, despite the sun now shining and bringing color into the soaring windows of the great hall, there was still a grayness, a bleak pall and the only sound came from the harp—that disturbing, monotonous three-note tone. The clap of hooves on the stones kept time.

At the eastern end of the hall Wulfstan and Richildis sat in chairs of state on a dais surrounded by their courtiers as George made his slow progress, pausing every ten paces to lower his beribboned lance in tribute. From where she stood with Petronelle in a gallery high above him, Joanna wished George would look up; that small gesture would prove to her that all was well.

George dismounted at the dais steps and walked up to kneel before Wulfstan. He offered his sword and a token of his battles—a single dragon tooth, placing them on the pavement. Richildis came forward now holding a magnificent cup and offered it to George.

"The champion must drink from this cup. Twenty-one years have passed since it was forged and beaten from a lump of gold from the Holy Land," Wulfstan pronounced. "It was to be a wedding cup, but now our champion and savior drinks from it, for we are wedded to him for his labor and give him great thanks."

George hesitated but the cold metal of the rim was at his mouth.

"You've earned this victory," Richildis whispered and all but forced him to take the cup.

Joanna watched as George took a long drink and felt as if all the air had been sucked out of her. In three days of trials and danger, of uncertainty, she had not been so fearful of death until that moment. That fear made her heart race when figures moved from the shadows of the hall and surrounded George as soon as he handed the cup back to Richildis.

"Who are these knights?" Joanna whispered to Petronelle. "I've never seen them before!"

"Who? Those by the screen?" Petronelle asked,

looking in another direction.

It was as Joanna feared; once again, only she could see George's demons. They were eight in number and all gray and blue in color, the pallor of death had lain on them for many years. They were whispering a prayer, "*Libere me Domine*." Joanna was certain only she and George could hear the chant.

"Joanna, what is it?" Petronelle demanded.

The music grew louder and more disturbing as George rose to his feet, and not without difficulty. While Wulfstan read a proclamation, George started to sway unsteadily. He gasped for air and pulled at the gorget around his neck and threw it to the ground. The clatter of metal against stone was a relief from the music. Then he started unbuckling the chain mail, his hands trembling and his face bathed in sweat.

He fell, tumbling down the steps where he lay at Roger and Adam's feet.

✠ ✠ ✠

"LORD WULFSTAN DEMANDS an audience!" Stephen hissed at Joanna. She back glared at him and blocked the entrance to George's bedchamber.

"And I tell you the earl of Grasmere is in no fit state to receive anyone—even if the blessed Archangel Michael came back to do more battle!" Joanna growled. "It is because of your master that he lies in bed and will not get up! Come tomorrow and we'll see if he is fit!"

Joanna slammed the door on him and put hands to her ears, sick of the strange music that continually filled the hallways and chambers of the castle. More than that, she was weary of this strange place and wanted the familiarity of home—even if she didn't really have one.

"How much longer do you think he'll sleep?" Petronelle asked, looking up from her vigil on George's ashen face. She leaned over and brushed a stray curl from his forehead.

"I don't know," said Joanna.

"I've seen this—men sleeping after battle for days, weeks at a time. Some never wake," Roger added. He poured a cup of ale and offered it to Joanna, who drank and then put the cup to George's lips with the hope that would wake and drink.

"They poisoned him."

Adam's statement was forthright, his sentence finished by Petronelle. There was no other way to explain it; the intervening minutes between his drinking from the cup and his collapse on the sanctuary steps had been few. There could be no explanation. A celebration became a death watch for Petronelle.

"Why can't we just take him back to Skelwith? We could carry him out and no one would know; they're so deep in their cups!" Petronelle demanded bitterly.

"With all the strange goings-on, do you think it would be that easy?" Adam argued.

"I would never be forgiven if I allowed George to die here!" she snapped.

"He isn't going to die!" Joanna cried. "Why is everything final with you? Can you not see how strong your brother is?"

"Were that so, Joanna Fletcher, he would have risen from bed two days ago and fought his way out of this place!" growled Petronelle.

"Why did you come if you have so little faith?"

Joanna demanded, coming around the bed to face her. "Did you truly desire to see your brother honor a pledge, or was it convenient so that you could run from a marriage you didn't want?"

Petronelle raised a hand to strike Joanna, but Roger took the hand and forced it to the angry girl's side, holding it fast in his own.

A knock on the door ended their quarrel. Roger looked at both women and Adam and put a finger to his lips for silence. When Roger gave Adam the signal, he opened the door. Lord Wulfstan and Lady Richildis entered and stopped just short of the bed.

"What do you want?" Petronelle snapped.

"We've brought medicines; herbs of the North Country that are known to heal a man in this state," Richildis said as she handed Petronelle an alabaster jar, though she looked straight at Joanna. "He will be fit to ride with us tomorrow morning."

"Ride where?" Petronelle and Joanna demanded.

Offering a perfunctory courtesy—but no answer—they were gone.

The vigil went on for another two hours before Adam looked at the jar Petronelle had set on a shelf over the bed. "Nothing else has worked," he sighed. He poured water into a cup and then added a sprinkling of the herbs, watching the leaves and stems float on top of the water and then slowly sink. Adam was about to administer the potion when Joanna leapt to her feet and snatched the cup. "No!" Joanna cried. She tossed the liquid into the hearth where it extinguished the fire. "God knows what they've given him! Do you not wonder why everyone here is sullen, why everyone moves as if in a deep slumber? George has destroyed something evil and yet there is worse evil still here!"

"It may be a restorative," Adam countered. "I tell you, nothing else has worked!"

"And I tell you it is something evil!"

Petronelle sat upright and looked closer at her brother's face, where a gray pallor was beginning to spread from neck to brow. She glanced at Joanna in panic and knew. In her mind's eye, she saw the courtiers and soldiers of the court, and she put the pieces together.

"George isn't the first, or the last," she said. "You knew. You saw! God forgive me for doubting you, Joanna. I think every man in Eskeleth has championed Wulfstan and his daughter and drank from that cup. I think the sooner we take him from here, his chances of surviving will improve."

"A maiden's fanciful imagination from reading ancient romances," Roger scoffed as he took a cup of wine.

"Is it?" Adam wanted to know. "When you consider all that's passed, I mean to say, well, it stands to reason . . ."

"The water from the spring is a restorative," Joanna said, as she bathed George's face. "If I could go to the coppice."

"I won't allow it. If George was in a better state, he wouldn't allow it, either," Roger stated flatly.

"We talk and talk, we argue, and what do we do? Nothing that helps him," Joanna muttered. Then, in a louder voice, "You saw what the water can do. And the apples, if I could,"

"Did you hear me, girl? I said no!"

"Whatever evil was there is gone! I don't see how,"

"That's what Wulfstan would like us to believe. Make no step towards that place, Mistress Fletcher, for I am certain that place will be George's death or yours!" Joanna was ready with an argument but Roger shook his head. "Not another word!"

Each went to a corner of the chamber and settled in for the night. Petronelle and Roger cuddled on a window seat and Adam stretched out before the hearth hoping to find some heat from the dying embers. Joanna sat by the bed and kept watch over George.

The bells tolling midnight disturbed George's sleep and he thrashed about, muttering about fires and ships and going to the safety of the lighthouse. Gently she brushed the sweat damp curls off his forehead and whispered consolation but her actions did little. She took a bowl from the table and poured water from the ewer. She knew it would be hopeless to bathe his hands and face once again. The ghastly pallor of death and the bouts of sweating would not be held at bay. Reaching over to tuck the blankets around George, one of the balls of thread rolled from her surcote pocket onto the pillows. Joanna reached out to retrieve it and gasped. There was a change in George's appearance and breathing. Spots of color appeared on his face and his shallow death rattles were slow, deep, relaxed breaths. When she moved the thread the gray pallor and the painful, labored breathing returned.

"Roger! Petronelle! Adam! Come and see!' she whispered to the others but they were all fast asleep.

Joanna grabbed the ball and went in search of Osprey. She found him sitting alone by the fire in the great hall. He looked up and smiled when he heard her footsteps.

"Why do you help him?" Joanna demanded as she halted before his chair. "You have tormented him all his life and you brought him here! Tell me why!"

"I would help any man in his place. He is the first and only to have achieved what others could not," Osprey said, winking.

"You're their creature – I don't believe you!"

"You of all people have no belief?"

"Don't play with me, old man! I'm not a goose girl or whore!"

"Why then do you ask? I know who you are and who your father is. Because of your father you understand more than you let on and keep the secrets close. That is your armor. The earl of Grasmere is not so fortunate in his. That is why I chose to help him. He should not have had to pay the blood debt. The sin was never his. You understand that."

Joanna slumped wearily at his feet. "What I don't understand is why all this bother. You might have done something in Grasmere."

Osprey laughed but not in derision. "The journey is often more important than the destination." He leaned forward and patted her cheek. "For reasons I cannot tell, I cannot tell you all, but this. I help George because he is my grandson." He chuckled at the look of shock Joanna gave him, and winked. "A promise has been kept, a debt repaid, a challenge accepted and won - use what words you will to explain it to others. Just be sure to act immediately and take him from this place."

Now Joanna held out the thread. "This. It has a good and perhaps holy power. Give me the means to make it into something for I know it will protect him."

Crooking a finger at her, Osprey now leaned towards a small table at his left and opened the cask upon it, taking a pair of needles. "It will protect you both."

✠✠✠

"THERE'S NO HOPE for it! She's gone mad with grief!" Petronelle growled as Roger pounded on Joanna's chamber door. They'd been there for almost an hour and still Joanna would not respond to the raps, the knocks, the pounding and pleading.

Three days had passed since she confronted Osprey. Joanna locked herself up in the bedchamber and worked tirelessly on a banner made of the thread, refusing both food and company. When she finally emerged the banner was wrapped about her neck and shoulders as a scarf or shawl might, its bright colors a fascinating pattern of blues, yellows, purples, reds and greens to an unknowing eye. Joanna went straight away to George's chamber and to the bed to check on his progress.

"What a curious girl you are, Joanna. What are you about?" Petronelle wanted to know and fingered the silken fabric around her neck. Joanna paid no attention and wiped George's sweating face with the hem of the banner. No one saw the faint smile that crossed his lips.

"We are guests of Lord Wulfstan, not his hostages," Joanna said, turning to her companions.

"George has paid his father's debt in full, don't you think? I am willing to bid farewell to Eskeleth tonight. Who will come with me?"

"I will," Adam spoke up.

"And I," Roger added. "Lady Petronelle, what say you?"

"Aye; we can carry George on a litter."

"Make everything ready. Before we leave, there is one thing left for me to do," Joanna said and slipped out of the chamber as quickly as arrived. Roger sputtered a protest and turned to the others growling, "Be about your business and see that all is done! I'm going to see what mischief she's caught in."

Roger left in time to see Joanna stop Osprey as he climbed the donjon stairs, taking his hand and allowed the old man to lead her out of the castle. He stormed back to the bedchamber and took up his sword. "False little witch!" Roger growled to himself, but Petronelle heard and stopped bundling George in blankets. "What are you saying? Who?"

"Joanna! She's in league with them! I saw it for myself! She's enchanted George. That would explain a lot. She'll pay dearly for this betrayal!"

Petronelle stopped Roger at the door, Adam joining her. "You cannot be certain! It's obvious she loves George and my brother surely has some regard for Joanna."

"And what better way to disarm and conquer and ruin a man than the ruse of love!"

"You speak from experience?" Petronelle demanded.

"By all the saints, Petra, I did not mean you, or us!"

"I do not think Joanna as cruel and deceitful as that cold witch Richildis even if you do! I trust Joanna and I trust George's life with her!"

"As do I," Adam swore.

Their argument continued until Joanna returned with her cloak bundled like a sack. One look at the girl with cheeks rosy and eyes bright and Roger grabbed her by the shoulders and shook her as if she were a small child.

"It's not enough that we're near to losing George," Roger bellowed at the girl; "but now's not the time to make rapprochements with the enemy! I saw you with him! You were with that old man! God's life, what were you thinking?"

As Roger continued to shake her, apples fell from her cloak and escaped over the floor. A full wineskin thudded softly at their feet.

Joanna twisted free. "Leave off, you great fool! I was getting provisions—these are better than any medicine—water from the spring, and apples. You won't believe me if I tell you, but I'll tell you all the same. Osprey is George's grandfather!" When no one spoke, she continued. "He is the father of the girl Aubrey betrayed. He came to help George as much as we did. Now leave off and let us go home!"

The sound of an apple falling and rolling towards the bed rent the painful, embarrassed silence. When Roger made ready to speak and apologize, Joanna turned on him angrily.

"God forgive you, sir, for what you thought of me!"

Muttering an apology, Roger moved away and started picking up the apples.

✠✠✠

IT WAS THE MOST difficult thing they had done, carrying George down the spiral staircases of the Golden Tower on a litter made of sheets and the staffs of hauberks. The litter was jostled and bumped, and twice they almost lost hold of it, nearly losing their footing on staircases poorly lit with oil lamps, all the while trying not to be discovered. Once they reached the gallery to the great hall, Roger said, "Take him to the stables and find a wagon and horses. Get everything ready to leave—and try to be quick and unseen. I'll meet you there, and for God's sake, be ready to leave at a moment's notice!"

He walked unhindered into the hall, where four great tables were spread with enough food to feed all of the dales, and the guests dined quietly while the strange, disturbing music played and a courtier read from Leviticus. Roger stopped before the dais where Wulfstan sat with Richildis and their retainers.

"Wulfstan of Eskeleth!" Roger shouted over the music and drone of recitation after several tries.

Wulfstan raised a hand for silence.

"What do you require of us?" Wulfstan asked quietly.

"Leave to return to Cumbria, my lord. To bring our friend and brother home. If he is to die, let it be in his own bed."

"He made a promise," Richildis started, rising to her feet.

"None to you, my lady; we all witnessed his fulfillment of a promise made by Lord Aubrey, and indeed, you saw for yourself that he was able to do what no knight before him could accomplish."

"He made a promise!" she spat, coming from the table.

"Are we not your guests?" Roger demanded. "Why should you hold us against our will?"

"It was agreed!" Richildis hissed now, coming even closer. "His father and mine made a contract."

"And my lord of Grasmere has honored that contract, has he not?" Roger answered calmly.

"There is a pledge that has not been redeemed. I made an oath to my kinswoman on the day she died that I would see it done! It was the pledge Aubrey of Grasmere dishonored, and necessitated our work here."

"Your work, Lady? Whatever labor that might be, again I say to you, Grasmere has made good his father's name."

"When he stands before the Bishop of Cumbria and makes a solemn pledge of marriage, then I will say that Ascalon of Grasmere's debt has been paid in full!"

"I am concerned, my lady, that you have done something more than what was agreed upon."

"Your concerns are unfounded," Wulfstan spoke up.

"Are they, my lord? Why did the earl of Grasmere fall ill after you bade him drink from the cup? Why is there still no life in Eskeleth, when beyond the gates all is green and the air is fresh, and here everything is decayed, stale, and stinks beyond understanding?"

"You go too far!"

"We are your guests and we will now take our leave."

"I forbid it!" Richildis screamed.

"Hold us against our will and you will answer to the king!"

Lord Wulfstan's knights drew their swords and waited for the command. Roger glanced around the hall and saw that he had no champion. "You will answer to the king," Roger repeated. "Let us leave quietly, and now, and it will be said that Wulfstan of Eskeleth is a man of his word. Honors will be granted for the service done today."

"Father! My lord, I beg you not to entertain this request! You know what shame Ascalon has brought on us!" Richildis whispered angrily at Wulfstan.

"You must give up this quest, Richildis," Wulfstan said low; "George Ascalon has been honorable, and it will do us no good to insist on what I did agree to— no, speak not a word more! We can gain what we seek by being agreeable!" Then in a loud voice he said for the benefit of the courtiers and knights assembled, "We would not dare anger his grace the king, and know that Grasmere is his liegeman. Sir, you may go with your party, but see that you go quickly—before I change my mind." Waving his hand, Wulfstan bade the musicians play. The music started up and the courtier continued to drone passages of scripture. The guests continued to eat and drink as if the little drama had not just played out.

Roger skirted out of the hall and ran as fast as he could to the stables where Adam, Petronelle, and Joanna waited, having done all that had been required of them. Adam waited on the wagon seat, his hands trembling as they waited to snap the reins and be gone. George was bundled in the wagon bed and slept soundly, Petronelle beside him.

As soon as Joanna saw Roger she rode forward, leading another horse that he leapt upon and wheeled about towards the gate. "Let us be gone now!" he cried hoarsely.

Digging heels into the flanks of horses, snapping the reins, they set off. Adam drove the wagon through the gate first, followed by Joanna, then Roger. No one looked at the coppice as they rode past; they didn't see how the trees were top heavy with fruit and the spring had grown in length and reached to the gate that Roger galloped through, stopping at the gray, stark walls of Eskeleth.

Nor did they see Richildis standing at an oriel in the Golden Tower, but they heard her screams, the ancient prayers from the old ways that she chanted and her cries for vengeance for more than a mile distant from the cursed place.

CHAPTER 16

R OGER PUSHED ADAM and the girls to ride hard and fast so that by daybreak they had arrived in Keld, the last town before the Cumbrian marches, entering the market square just as the tradesmen and farmers were setting up their stalls. A great mountain made of bales of wool caught Adam's eye and he steered the wagon toward it. It was far enough away from the stalls and market cross that they could rest undisturbed.

"How is it with him?" Roger asked, dismounting. He leaned into the wagon and tucked the blankets around George, who slept soundly despite their breakneck jaunt.

"He's been talking in his sleep," Petronelle said. "Something about fires and Constantinople, a child lost and his mother, soldiers."

"The crusade," Adam murmured. He took the water skin from Roger and poured a little on a rag, using it to wipe George's face. "He looks better; he's not as ashen as before and his breathing is even. How far is it to Grasmere now?"

"Another three days, four if the weather goes against us. Adam, come with me to find something to eat; ladies, wait here, but, take these—just in case," Roger handed Petronelle a dagger, which she quickly placed up her sleeve, and gave Joanna George's sword. After a last look at George, Roger went off in search of breakfast with Adam in tow.

Joanna dismounted wearily and lowered herself gingerly onto one of the wool bales. "You ought to rest," Petronelle remarked, sitting beside her.

"I think we'll not sleep easy until the walls of Skelwith Castle are in sight," Joanna yawned, "and George is safe in his own bed."

"We were right to take him away from that place," Petronelle sighed. She glanced at her brother and reached over to brush hair off his face. "My sweet George; what did they do to you? You mustn't give up!"

"This cloth protects him," Joanna murmured as she rearranged the banner tucked underneath the blanket covering George.

Petronelle saw the design embroidered on the silk-like fabric and kept Joanna from covering it. "How beautiful!" she exclaimed. "Here is a knight and his lady – though a sword separates them, they clasp hands. Is this the apple tree in the coppice?" Petronelle traced the outline of the figures. Just so, they were of a knight and his lady, a sword between them and they stood under a flowering tree.

"There is a garden on the roof of the donjon of the Golden Tower. This is a rose bush. We met there before the contest," Joanna said, embarrassed.

"And this is the sword of Ascalon!"

"Yes," Joanna now pointed to the Greek letters spelling out ASCALON in gold thread on the hems of the banner. "It was as if the thread wove and embroidered itself and I was merely a guide. Once I started, I could not stop, except to pray at times and I always felt – it is no matter now. It's done."

"As if an angel protected you?" Petronelle urged, smiling.

"Yes, but I could not speak of it to anyone. No one believed me."

Petronelle embraced Joanna tearfully. "I would! I have seen that angel!"

They wept out of relief and fear in the others' arms, venting weeks of anxiety. Joanna broke away and turned to the cart to clasp George's hand. "Whatever demons plagued George before, he is watched by God and His angels, I'm certain of it; and I pray that he will live," she said.

"I'm not so certain about you, Joanna!" Petronelle commented when Joanna swayed from fatigue and grabbed the wagon side for support. "Come, there's room enough in the wagon, and it will be a comfort to him."

"Leave me!" Joanna protested. "It's the heat of the day, naught else."

"You're as gray as death. Now come do as you're bid—by the evangels and saints! How could this be?" she exclaimed.

"Petronelle and Joan both ducked out of sight when they recognized the livery of the knights riding into the square—Lord Wulfstan's men.

"They have no right to follow us!" Petronelle exclaimed in a whisper.

"Right or no, it doesn't matter."

"Lord, they come this way!"

Petronelle slipped the dagger from her sleeve and clenched it in her fist; Joanna grabbed George's sword and made ready. They crouched behind the wagon, so that they could see the legs and boots of the two knights that had dismounted and were approaching the wagon.

"This is the cart, I know the markings," one knight said to the other. "Let's see what's here."

As the knight lifted the blanket off George's face, Petronelle leapt up and thrust the dagger at the man's neck. Joanna leveled her weapon at the men, who were both taken by surprise.

"He's dead. What more can you ask of him?" Petronelle growled. "Be on your way!"

"The cart belongs to my lord Wulfstan of Eskeleth," said one knight. "Carry him on your shoulders if you must; the wagon comes with us."

"And I say leave be!" Petronelle hissed. "What's one cart to Wulfstan? He got his use out of Grasmere. The debt is paid!"

"Maybe you have something to offer, sweetheart?" the second knight suggested to Petronelle with a wink of an eye.

And then, for the first time in days, George stirred and opened his eyes. This didn't go unnoticed by the girls. Petronelle moved in front of the wagon to block the knights' view, making it seem as though she was afraid of the knight's suggestion, and as George tried to move, Joanna climbed into the wagon, throwing herself on George.

"Oh my poor lord! How shall I survive without you? You made a promise to marry me!" Joanna carried on. "What will become of me? Our child!"

"Now see what you've done?" Petronelle scolded. "She was all dried up with tears this morning, and was ready to bid him farewell, and you remind us of what

Grasmere sacrificed for that cold, hard-hearted bitch you call a lady!"

"Either we take the wagon—or you, mistress!" the second knight said, leering. "For my part, you can keep the wagon."

"Gentlemen!"

Joanna stopped her wailing at the sound of Roger's voice and sat up, gently freeing herself of George's weak grasp. Roger and Adam pushed their way through the spectators that had gathered.

"What happy chance is this!" Roger greeted the knights. "Did your lord commission you to escort us to Skelwith?"

"I suppose they knew my lord of Grasmere would die on the road and have come to give him a fitting escort to his grave," Joanna started in again, sobbing and throwing herself on George. "He grows cold! My poor love! My lord! What's to become of me? The child! The child, my lord!" While she wailed and keened, she looked out through the tangle of her loose hair and winked at the horrified Adam and amused Roger.

"Aye," Roger said, nodding. "It would be the honorable thing to do."

"I think we're fitting enough to escort Grasmere home, don't you, lady Petronelle?" Adam spoke up.

"Agreed. Why should we accept the service of those who would do us harm?" Petronelle said as she scrambled up, sitting on top of her brother to keep him still. "Tell your mistress and lord that Grasmere has paid its debt in full and wants no more of Eskeleth."

"The wagon!" the first knight growled.

"It will be returned," Roger promised. "We'll go now, and without another word from you." He nodded towards the Keld watch, who were standing on the perimeter of the crowd. "You have no power here, and even if you did, Grasmere has Keld's allegiance. Go on."

The knights gave the wagon a last look and then retreated. It wasn't until they had disappeared into the growing crowd in the market that Adam scrambled onto the wagon seat, Roger following.

"You choose your moments, don't you, George?" Roger whispered, and snapped the reins crisply so that the horses shied and whinnied, eager to get going. He winked at Joanna and said, "A fine performance, mistress!"

"Why do we have to fly like criminals?" Adam demanded as they set off, careening towards the road out of Keld.

"Lord Wulfstan keeps a foul magic around him, there's no telling what he might do, or what he's done already; truth be told, we've more to fear from his daughter. We'll be gone and there's an end. Hold tight now!"

They were soon speeding west. By the end of their third day on the road, they were closer to Grasmere and spirits began to rise, especially when George began to speak.

"Where are we?" he whispered.

"Somewhere between the north country and the lakes," Petronelle offered, placing a cup to his lips. George froze and clamped his mouth shut like a small child refusing medicine. "No Brother!" Petronelle laughed. "This is water from the spring. Joanna filled a wineskin and brought apples, too. See?" She held up a perfect, round, blood-red apple that glistened in the early morning sun. He relaxed and nodded, allowing Petronelle to give him a drink.

"Joanna?" he asked now.

"Riding before us, with Roger."

George reached out and took her hand, made an effort to kiss it. Petronelle laughed softly and returned the kiss, saying, "The hand you ought to kiss is Joanna's—she's saved your life in so many ways."

"Where do we go?"

"We're going home," said Petronelle softly.

"I have a pledge to keep—to return without honoring—"

"Don't you remember?" Petronelle's voice raised with concern. "We went to Eskeleth, in Arkengarthdale. You killed the dragon. And now we're going to Little Langdale, where you can rest and regain your strength."

"The hiding place—I put it there," George whispered.

"And it will be there when you return—whatever it is. Now go to sleep; it's not far to home." Petronelle cradled his head in her lap and smoothed his hair, singing a cradle song from their childhood.

George smiled faintly and said, "You'd rather it was Roger here, eh, Petra?"

"And you would rather I was Mistress Fletcher!"

"We deserve to be happy."

A day later as they approached the border between the north country and the west they were met by three Benedictines standing at the roadside. The tallest of them stepped out into the wagon's path and blocked its way.

"God grant you a good day, Brothers," Roger greeted, sidling up with Joanna at his side. "Do you wish alms?"

"We wait for George Ascalon," the tallest brother spoke up.

"You've found him," Petronelle said. "But he's in no state to speak. Perhaps if there's a priest among you, you may give him the blessed sacrament?"

"Indeed," the stout brother in the trio said. "The church is there—you can just see the bell tower among the trees."

"Roger, let us put in at the church for a bit," Petronelle instructed.

St. Bryde's Abbey stood directly outside the town walls of Wattle, and those town walls were crowded with well-wishers who erupted into cheers and singing as soon as George's party came into sight. It took patience and effort to hold the people back as they brought George into the abbey church and laid his pallet on the floor in front of the high altar.

"A fit place to be buried," George quipped. Petronelle and Joanna helped him sit upright and supported him as the brothers prepared the Eucharist. "Who are all those people?" George whispered and was heard by the stout brother.

"Your father charged us with giving you a safe rest on your journey home and so we bid you stay with us a time—and the townspeople wish to honor the knight who slew a dragon as in days of old," he explained.

A priest came from the sacristy and genuflected before the wooden crucifix on the wall above the altar.

"*In nomine Patris, et Filii, et Spiritus Sancti.* Amen."

A quietness settled on George as the priest recited the words of the mass and those kneeling protectively around him whispered the responses. When had he last heard mass? George could not remember. He closed his eyes and listened, his mind's eye seeing the poor chapel at the Golden Tower, the roses blooming in the urns, the paintings and icons of saints and angels glowing brightly, the silhouette of Joanna in the dusky light as they prayed together. Warmth like the sun enfolded him and tears began to bead on his eyelashes, gliding down his cheeks.

"I will receive!" George gasped as the priest broke a loaf of bread and chanted the Agnus Dei.

And then the priest came from around the altar and past the rood screen through the quire to where George lay. He paused only a moment and knelt down, whispering the words of Communion as George took both elements. It took all the strength left in him to raise his mouth for the bread, to put his lips to the chalice; it was like another contest, but this time there was no evil, only exquisite love that drained him and left him breathless.

He fell into a restful, healing sleep then and woke the next morning alone in one of the guest houses. The scent of the linen sheets; the soft woolen covers; and the pale, whitewashed walls of the bedchamber decorated with devotional panels of the Virgin and child were as comforting and welcoming as the soft bed. He turned over in bed and burrowed into the pillows, deciding to take another hour's sleep. God knew he deserved it! As he settled in, George saw the banner draped over a chest. A shaft of sunlight rested on the fine silk cloth, making the two figures of man and woman glow as if living and breathing creatures. The sword between them as bright as any weapon newly crafted, the rose bushes heavy with rich, red, blossoms and green foliage.

George shoved the blankets off and sat up. Movement came easily and the dull, pounding headache that had plagued him for weeks was gone. Sliding out of bed, he went to the chest and made a careful inspection of the banner. He smiled and knew it was Joanna's work. He knew the restorative; he welcomed the cure.

George dressed and went out taking the banner with him, skirting past the other houses to avoid delay. He went into the church and was glad to see the priest offering the mass. Once again, George received the sacraments and that wonderful, now-familiar warmth took over. When he finally left the church as the bells rang the hour, he was surprised to find a crowd of townspeople on the steps, and that crowd let up a roar of excitement.

The happy noise was deafening and the crush of people frightening, yet George managed to negotiate his way through the happy crowd, his arms full of gifts, listening to the chanting of "Grasmere!" as if it were the comforting rhythm of a heartbeat.

✠✠✠

JOANNA THREW A two and a six. Adam groaned and scooped up the dice, avoiding her smile of victory. "That's seven times now," he sighed in mock disgust.

"Too bad you didn't throw a seven," Joanna teased. "That's three angels and tuppence, I think!"

Adam fished about in the scrip on his belt and dug out the coins, slapping them into Joanna's hand. "That's more money than you've seen in months, I wager," he quipped. "Will you buy some slippers or a new gown in the market at Little Langdale?"

"No," she said, glancing out the window. "I'll put it to better use. I'll buy masses."

Adam was going to remark that the dead didn't need the money, but saw that Joanna was looking out towards the chapel, watching George as he was greeted by yet more well-wishers from the town and took more gifts. A young mother held up her infant for George to kiss, which he did with some embarrassment. Joanna was going to buy prayers for George's well-being, and if there was ever a soul that was in need of divine intervention, it was George Ascalon.

"Praise be to God, he's on his feet at last; Roger was telling us yester evening that if he didn't heal soon, he never would," said Adam as he joined her by the window. "Father Abbot said we will feast tonight in honor of the lord earl's victory over death. I think everyone from Keld to Wattle will sit down at table and rejoice, except the guest of honor. I don't know him half as well as others, but I know he wants to put it behind him."

"You know him quite well, Adam. I'll see you at supper," Joanna replied and smiled as she left the guest house. She walked towards the cloister and stood in the shadows as people continued to praise and congratulate George, who looked weary but nevertheless showed patience and courtesy. One little boy shoved a puppy in his arms and while George struggled to keep the dog safe as more people came forward, he saw her. He smiled and bade the townspeople a farewell, slipping through the colonnades to where Joanna waited, stopping just short of where she stood, wanting to take her in his arms but feeling compelled for the first time not to take such a liberty.

"You've enchanted even a puppy," she said, smiling.

"Yours, if you want it," George responded, holding the little bundle of soft, tawny fur out to Joanna.

"Thank you!" Joanna answered with delight and took the puppy. She scratched behind its silky ears and whispered endearments before looking up at George and asking, "How is with you, my lord?"

"My name is George," he teased, adding, "And I feel as if I've been sleeping for years."

"Days, more like."

"I can't remember—is this new?" George said, holding out the banner. "It seems familiar."

"I made it to celebrate your victory. It was Petronelle's idea."

"Is this us?" He pointed at the figures and let his thumb and forefinger cover their clasped hands.

"A knight and his lady. Yes, I suppose. I was compelled to make it, to make the design – it tells the story of George Ascalon. Not the entire story,"

"Doesn't it?" he asked softly and draped the banner around her. She gazed at the cloth around her neck and shoulders and smiled.

"I wore it when I'd finished the work, and I placed it on your bed while you slept. I feel protected when I wear it. It makes me feel close."

"To what?"

"It doesn't matter," she answered, blushing.

"Did we really go to Eskeleth?"

"Well, here's a scar that proves it," she answered, touching the red, rough patch on her left hand where she had held a sword.

He kissed the hand.

"There are scars a person cannot see, my lady of Merioneth," George murmured and with a finger traced the crucifix she wore in the hollow between her breasts, that finger trembling as he touched the velvet-like skin, her breath coming quicker.

"And those were made long ere you came to this."

"I came home to . . . well, it doesn't matter now. All that matters is going home."

"To become a gentleman farmer," she teased.

"A noble profession. Planting seed and watching it grow to barley and wheat so that it will eventually make bread and I can feed the hungry."

"Will you be happy, George?" she whispered softly.

"He reached out and brushed a curl off her cheek. "If you are there, yes."

She leaned a little closer, saying, "Yours—if you want it." And then she kissed him.

Gently he pulled her into his arms, and they held each other in a tentative embrace despite the powerful emotion roiling through both of them and until the puppy began to squeal and yelp from its close quarters and reminded them of where they were. Joanna broke away first, but George sought her again.

"Of all the people I choose to love," he whispered between kisses.

"My lord!"

The abbot's greeting ended the tryst. George turned and nodded as Father Abbot approached, but keeping Joanna in his line of sight and hoping she would stay.

"Father Abbot, My friends and I thank you for your hospitality," said George.

"Would you come and see the preparations for the feast tonight? I would that all is made ready according to your requirements," the abbot suggested.

"As you will, Father. My sister and friends deserve this more than I."

The abbot nodded and extended a hand towards the refectory. The sound of light footsteps on the pavement confirmed to George's dismay that Joanna had disappeared into one of the guest houses.

✠✠✠

THE PUPPY SNIFFED and explored the bedchamber, wagging its stub of a tail and trotting over to the bed whenever Joanna offered a scrap of food.

"I'll call you George," she said to the puppy as it came sniffing for more. "It's likely you're all I'm to have of him." Scooping him up, she rolled onto her back and held the little fellow aloft, letting him lick her face and then eat bits of food from her hand. "What becomes of a lady, George, whose dreams are in the clouds?"

"She dreams with angels."

The sound of his voice made Joanna's heart pound and she twisted about to see George standing by the door. Dropping the puppy, Joanna sat up and smoothed her hair back, adjusting the sleeves of her gown, feeling the color rise in her cheeks as she avoided looking at him. "Sometimes, foolishness is all that comes of dreams," she whispered.

"Sometimes, but not always." George came forward and lifted her chin with a forefinger, and tilting his head sideways, brows raised, he waited for an answer.

"I've received difficult lessons where it concerns dreams and disappointment. They are cruel sisters to me."

"How?"

"I should have died after my family was disgraced. Because I did not, I should never have left the cottage in Butcher's Lane."

"No! You shouldn't think that!" George said curtly. "Think instead how miserable it would have been to continue in that life, or worse, to be dead."

"I would not have aimed so high in expectation. I would not have gone on this journey with you. And I would not have fallen in love with someone I know I cannot have."

George knelt and kissed the hem of her dress. "I would not have had such a worthy champion at my side at the worst of times. I don't know what I would have done without that company." He reached up now and took her hands. "I cannot think, I will not think, of my life without your company!"

Joanna threw herself into his welcoming arms and whispered, "What's to become of us?" She didn't care if he answered, for the security of his presence, the strength of his arms, and knowing his love was all that mattered. Her question was still unanswered and of no moment hours later when they lay between the sheets and coverlet, drowsy and contented in an afterglow.

"How is it that you, of all people, could see my demons?" George asked suddenly, entwining the fingers of her hand with his. "When my sister, my childhood companion, and playmate, could not? When Roger, my closest friend for years, could not? People I thought were as close to me as I to them?"

"Petronelle was beginning to see them—in the great hall at Eskeleth, you see. After you drank from the cup. You cannot fault them; perhaps they have other struggles, other demons that they keep to themselves, just as you did," she answered. "And perhaps it has been so because my demons are not unlike yours. You were betrayed by those you love, sent off to crusade when you had neither heart nor stomach for war; I was betrayed by my father—he plotted against the king and would have been executed for treason, had he not escaped. I was left behind and was sold for a leman, first to the king and then to many more. Yet I understand and forgive him."

"That is how you came to Grasmere?"

"Bartered in exchange for a sheep!"

"A sacrificial lamb."

"Damaged goods, more like!"

"Not damaged, but precious like gold, a rare jewel."

Joanna laughed softly and planted a kiss on his lips. "Hopefully one that needs not be kept in a coffer or vault!"

"One that I would take to wife and wear gladly."

She gasped, genuinely surprised by the proposal. "Would you?" Joanna dared to ask.

"Given all that we've been through and shared, it would not be unseemly," George answered, kissing her. "And there is yet another reason, Mistress Fletcher. That is to say, I love no other but you."

"And I, you. But I think there is one battle left and it may be the most difficult for both of us."

"What more could we face as difficult as those we met in Eskeleth?"

Joanna kissed him hard, so that desire started to mount in both. She broke away and held his face in her hands. "You would have to seek consent from the king. I am the daughter of a presumed traitor and conspirator, and I am banished from court with a penalty of death. George, would you be willing to take on this uncomfortable yoke? To be safe only within your earldom? And what would you do if the king refused your suit and stripped you of lands and titles?"

"As I said," he whispered, leaning in, "what more could we face as difficult as the contests in Eskeleth? Besides, what are houses but stones, and what is land but acres of earth, compared to love? And the name and title sweetest to me is Joanna my wife!"

"Are you certain?"

"Here is proof!" he said breathlessly between kisses that grew deeper and more passionate. They sought one another amidst the tangle of bed linens and blankets, laughing softly as lips finally found their marks and the urgency to be as one grew stronger and overwhelmed them both.

"Give me your ring." Joanna said as they held

each other in another afterglow.

George slipped the ring of the lords of Grasmere off the great finger of his right hand and placed it in her palm. She reached behind her and untied the hair ribbons so that her heavy locks spilled down across her breasts and tickled George's face, took the crucifix and hung it from one of the ribbons and tied it around his neck. "Here is my pledge," she continued and looped the ring on the other ribbon, dropping it around her neck.

"So we are pledged," George said, smiling.

"So it must be," she said, kissing the ring.

CHAPTER 17

THE RING WAS a beacon for George later that evening, leading him to Joanna in the midst of the festivities as she danced with Roger first, and then Adam; as she sat with the ladies and whispered and laughed with Petronelle. It dangled on that ribbon around her slender neck and hid beneath her gown of rose-colored silk and blue surcote and the linen chemisette, lying next to dewy skin that George had kissed and wanted to kiss again, to lie next to as he fell asleep that night. Whenever their eyes met, George would draw the crucifix from under his shirt and kiss the cross that had touched her, and she would kiss the ring. It was a delightful game; George would be sure to suggest other games later . . .

"My lord? Your guests want to hear about your victory," the abbot was saying to George, who glanced up from his cup and from over the rim saw Joanna in animated conversation with Roger, their heads close, their smiles merry. George felt jealous all of a sudden, but that emotion was quelled when Joanna looked up and nodded demurely, though the look in her eyes was anything but.

"My lord?" said the abbot again.

"What's to tell?" George answered. "I repaid a debt owed by my father."

"Not in full, my lord of Grasmere!"

Richildis' voice set George's nerves on edge, and he dropped the cup, splashing wine on those seated nearest to him. He looked to the door, as did most of the guests. Richildis entered and made an obeisance as seductive as an Arabian dance. Roger and Petronelle were on their feet, bringing Joanna with them. As exquisite and beautiful as Richildis was, especially at that moment, all eyes were now set on George. He rose slowly, making sure not to let anyone see his discomfiture and coming around the table, squared off with her at a safe distance.

"Lady, why do you think so? Our fathers had an accord, which I honored," he answered quietly in a sure and calm voice, meeting her gaze. "You witnessed this. Let there be an end to this controversy. I've done what was required of me, and now I bid you leave me, leave us, in peace." He would have returned to his place had she not screamed and set the hairs on the back of his neck to stand on end.

"No! Not in full, I tell you! There is yet one debt unpaid!" Richildis shouted as she approached and opened her palm slowly. A golden button caught the candlelight. That was enough for George to grab Richildis by the arm and swing her around so that they faced one another, much too close for Joanna's liking.

George stared Richildis down, but even so, his heart was pounding and the dull headache had returned. His vision blurred and the room began to swim in hot, watery light.

Impossible, he thought; it was a bad dream, nothing more.

He involuntarily looked at Joanna, who was

staring, as was his sister, at his tunic and the space where a button had gone missing, the button Richildis held.

"You took me to your bed at Gawthorp and made sweet promises, offered such a complete seduction, that I now carry your child!"

"A lie!" George shouted. "Now you go too far! It's unbecoming, Lady Richildis, to spread such a lie!"

Richildis yanked her arm free and stepped back. Her smile mocked him. "Is it? Such little proof I hold. By autumn in the new year the proof will substantial! So it would seem that the houses of Grasmere and Eskeleth are at last united—unless you behave as your father and grandfather did in their time and spirit away in the dark of night to leave a woman scorned and angry and in a most dangerous condition!"

She threw the button and it sailed across the table to pelt Joanna on the cheek and draw blood.

"You'll have no satisfaction from me!" George hissed, hand on sword.

"I'll take satisfaction now!"

Richildis knelt at the fire pit before her and took three glowing coals from the grating.

"My lady! You surely will do harm to yourself!" the abbot cried, but made no further protest when her hand and fingers showed no sign of injury. Richildis began singing, the words to her song unintelligible to the listeners, who now began to cross themselves and whisper.

"A witch!"

"She's a sorceress—she knows the old ways!"

"This is witchcraft!"

"Silence!" the abbot shouted. "Shame come to

you for dishonoring a noble and great lady! Her father and her father's father bestowed chantries and religious houses—"

"See her for what she is—a witch!" Petronelle railed at the abbot.

It was then that Richildis spun about in a dance and started singing louder. As she did so, the coals began to emit a steam that rose up in billows to the roof of the refectory until it was as if fog from the lakes had overcome the room; sight was impossible. She stopped singing and the clouds of fog dissipated. In her hand were three golden spheres that spun slowly, allowing one to see images within them as if looking in a polished glass, or still water in bright sunlight. Try as he might to avert his eyes, George stared into the orbs, not pleased with what he saw. He drew his sword and swung it wildly, hoping it would find quarry in Richildis' breast, but that did not happen. The sword shivered as if it had met steel or stone. Richildis was ready and countered the blow with a swift retort. George barely had a chance to move out of the way when he saw the sword flash under her cloak. It was an ordinary sword until one looked at the tip. The sharp point was tinged with a purple substance as thick as honey and the scent sickening sweet. One cut, however slight, would surely cause instant death.

"My lady, this was not part of the bargain!" the abbot protested.

"You set a trap?" George hissed at him.

"She swore she only wanted to talk to you!"

"He made a promise!" Richildis shrieked and the scream was like crackling of lightning hitting a tree.

The refectory shook and shuddered as if an earthquake had hit and the oil lamps swayed dangerously against the woolen hangings.

The stench of sulfur and decay wafted in, replacing the homey, comfortable smells of food cooking and incense, of burning logs. Slowly, softly, the familiar and disturbing music followed.

"Get out!" George shouted at the assembly. "Adam! Roger! Clear the room—now!"

The music grew louder as Richildis began to chant. George recognized the words—his old nurse used to sing to him in the tongue of Wales. But these were not nursery lullabies, rather something dark and evil. The chanting became stronger, and the cacophony of music and words made some in the room stagger to the floor or keel over in a faint in their haste to escape. Roger, Adam, and some of the brothers dragged the fallen to safety.

"I said, leave!" George screamed at his sister and Joanna, who stood in a corner watching.

Richildis raised her hand ever so slightly, conjuring a spell that rooted them to the floor. "Watch them die!" she hissed. Vines started to wind up from the planks and twist around Petronelle's ankles and shins. Joanna, however, seemed impervious to the spell. Richildis hissed new spells that made no difference. Finally she snapped her fingers and Joanna flew into the air and was battered against the wall behind Petronelle. She fell unconscious. Richildis approached slowly, muttering, and stood over the girl.

"No!" Petronelle screamed.

Richildis drove her sword down on Joanna's

breast, only to have it broken in two, the girl untouched.

The gleam around Joanna's neck caught George's attention. His ring reflected a thread of light. George felt renewed and pushed forward again, his attacks stronger, his resolve twice as strong. Richildis keened and howled and started to chant again. She turned to the hearth again and just as quickly George emptied a pitcher of water on the coals so that they sizzled and hissed with steam, the fire extinguished. When she raised her hands to conjure again, George caught those hands, which managed to seize his sword, and struggled to keep them locked while they fought for control of the weapon. Even so, her strange incantations were more useful than the sword, and she broke free. Pointing towards George, she screamed, and he dove for protection under one of the tables.

Furniture was tossed like stones at him; the abbot's high-backed chair conveniently fell so that George could use it as a shield as Richildis conjured arrows of flame in his direction. He crawled, dragging the chair before him to where Petronelle stood, vines binding her in place, and was joined by Roger and Adam. To Adam he said, "Get my shield, the banner, too, and quickly!" He motioned now to a brother nearby. "Bring as much holy water as you can carry!" Adam and the brother scrambled out of the refectory, a lash of flame just missing their heads. "Go around to the other side, behind her," George said to Roger, "and wait for my signal!"

Smoke and sulfur filled the lungs and made it impossible to see or breathe. Roger wrapped himself in his cloak and crawled on hands and knees to the far end of the refectory near the kitchens, where Richildis stood. Her attention was diverted to movement in the corner where George protected the girls and where a brother had returned with a jug. Adam came back at the same time and handed over the banner and shield. George splashed holy water on his shield, sword, and doused both girls. As he expected, the vines withered and died and Petronelle was free. Joanna sat up, dazed.

"Where is he? Where's Roger?" Petronelle demanded.

"Petra! Stay where you are! Make no move!"

George's order was disobeyed, for Petronelle had escaped from the barrier and now ran to where Roger crouched. Richildis screamed wildly as Petronelle threw herself into Roger's arms, clinging to her lover as he leveled his sword, waiting for the next attack; those screams became more violent and deafening when George threw the banner around Joanna and kissed her passionately before sending the girl off to safety.

George kicked the chair out of the way and took a defensive stance as Richildis approached, her movements seductive and measured.

The smoke in the room began to swirl about so that George's vision was obscured. The sword was wrenched from his hands by an unseen force and George watched as it sailed hilt over blade over hilt and fell into a void. At the same time, he felt that familiar and awful sensation of being lifted in the air.

No! I've paid the debt! Let there be an end to all this!

Suddenly he was hurled and fell rapidly through a

shower of blinding white light, to a street in
Constantinople.

CHAPTER 18

THE SMOKE SWIRLED about him as George lay on the ground and tried to get his bearings. He was aware of people around him – they were speaking quickly and in hushed voices below the howls of a woman in childbirth.

George pushed himself up and found himself in a house somewhere on the outskirts of the city. The place was more like one of the crofts at home than the clean and bright houses of the Mediterranean. The room was dark and the air fetid with the stench of blood and sweat, perfume and cooking food. A child had been born; mewling wails as the infant sucked in first breaths. Strange that no one seemed to rejoice or speak – George remembered the happiness and the chatter of the midwives and ladies of the bedchamber when his sister was born, girl though she was. Perhaps the child was deformed? No relief came until the midwife carried out the swaddled infant. As soon as they were gone, the women set to the mother, combing her hair, washing her and singing and laughing now. Smoke billowed out from the hearth and made it impossible to see and when it dissipated George was in a street and met by a sun as blinding and hot as one could imagine streaming down on the cobblestones and glowing off whitewashed houses with bright red tiled roofs.

George knew this place. He looked about, waiting.

"My lord, why are you here?"

The whisper made George turn, but there was no one in the street. He heard a dog barking and looked in that direction; saw a woman spirit down another street.

Aurelia!

George ran, felt as if he was being pushed in her direction, and he knew what to expect when he came to a courtyard where a fountain trickled. Bright flowers caught the sun and nearly blinded him with their color. Aurelia was at the fountain with water jars that she filled slowly and methodically from a silver stream. While she performed this menial task, she sang a *virelai* of the Occitane troubadours.

"Aurelia?" he asked, though it wasn't his voice and he didn't move his lips. The words and the sound came from deep within. She stopped singing and looked up at him.

"It is you!" she spat. "I knew it from the first when I heard the bells."

"Bells? I don't understand . . ."

"Why did you return?" she asked angrily. "What more hurt could you offer up? Wasn't it enough that you left me to bear our son alone?"

He came closer, fearful that she would dissolve like the smoke, or transform as she had done during his quest. The hand looked real enough, as did her round, dark eyes that reflected his image in them. George took the hand and was relieved that it was warm, and made of flesh and bone. Aurelia kissed his hand and George felt a searing pain, though he could not bring himself to pull away, nor did he cry out.

"Why are you still here?" he demanded. "I told you to leave with your husband!"

"He is dead," Aurelia answered him matter-of-factly, as if it was a query about a lost slipper. "I thought you would return. I waited, and then I gave up hope. I had nowhere to go. This is my home, after all."

"I would have stayed behind, Aurelia,"

"Would you? Some decisions were not ours to make; you of all people should know that," Aurelia said. She smiled sadly then. "If you had stayed, they would have found you and killed you for a traitor." Pausing to fill a jar and then wiping the lip carefully, Aurelia shook her head. "It was never to be. My husband had the final say. I still have the scar."

As she spoke, Aurelia unwound the scarf around her neck and revealed an ugly, festering wound where a knife had sliced. George reached up and touched it, feeling no pulse. "If you're dead, then—"

"—and our son. He would not suffer Julian to live." She stepped aside to reveal a cradle sitting on the pavement. In it was the child George had seen so many times before in his dreams. The baby smiled and reached for him. George picked him up and let the child explore his face with chubby fingers, studying him with large, round, blue eyes.

"My son," George laughed, and the baby howled as he returned the child to his mother. More seriously, he touched Aurelia's cheek and was alarmed at how cold it was. "Forgive me all the hurt I caused, my sins are too many to be counted, especially against you and Julian."

"What are promises compared to eternal life?"

she asked and tiptoed to kiss him. The touch of her lips was burning cold, almost as if he had touched ice. Then she whispered, "Tell me what you saw, George!"

"What do you mean?"

"Just now. In the mist and smoke. No one looks and is satisfied by what they see. It disturbs their minds and hearts. You saw a child being born to that woman. You saw it being taken away in secret."

"A bastard brat more than likely —"

"*You* were that child!"

George tried to stop her with kisses but Aurelia began to weep then, and the baby between them fretted. George tried to comfort her, and felt her tears soaking his tunic, felt the baby go limp as if sleeping, and then Aurelia shrieked in agony. He looked down and saw that she was gone, his son was gone, and his tunic was soaked in blood. Richildis was clutching at him, gasping and clawing as she crumpled into a heap on the floor. George looked up and saw Petronelle behind her, holding his bloodied sword.

No one moved. Roger was panting for breath and the mayor had come from the corner holding a pitchfork, stepping carefully over the broken bodies and furniture. The brothers began to creep back in when they were sure Richildis of Eskeleth was dead.

The silence. What was more frightening than what they had done was the silence.

Next came freedom. It suddenly became easier to breathe, to see, to move.

"George? George, your hand," Petronelle whispered.

He looked at his hands. The right was sliced

across the palm and bleeding. He clenched it and let drops fall on Richildis' body as he tested his reflexes, making sure there was no other damage.

"The debt is paid, Brother!"

Petronelle's whisper made him take her in a long, loving embrace. When he heard her soft weeping and felt her trembling, George held her even tighter.

CHAPTER 19

W HERE IS JOANNA?" George demanded once quiet had settled on the refectory and Richildis was carried to the abbey church. The brothers, Roger, Adam, and Petronelle all looked up from their cleaning and glanced about. "Did anyone see her?" he wanted to know when no one responded.

"You sent her away," Petronelle remarked absently. She pushed the hair off her face as she stepped over an overturned chair to retrieve trenchers and goblets and found George's ring on a ribbon among them. She held it out. George feared the worst as he took it and hurried back to the guest houses, ignoring the questions and voiced concerns of the brothers and guests as he passed. She wasn't in her chamber. Her belongings were untouched; a book lay open on the bed. The puppy scampered from his basket to see if George had anything to eat and walked away disinterested when he was ignored, looking up as the door slammed behind the man as he fled.

She was asleep in the abbey church. Upon entering the quire, George was approached by Osprey, a finger first to his lips, and then pointing to the stalls behind the altar. Joanna was curled up on a bench, her cheek resting against her hands like a child in slumber.

"Be at ease, George; she merely sleeps," Osprey said in a low and gentle voice. His eyes slid to the makeshift bier where Richildis lay before the altar in the center of the nave. "For three generations have we been at war with Cumbria and now we will know peace."

"I've conquered my demons," George murmured as he knelt before Joanna and gently bussed her cheek with a kiss. "I had no thought or care for myself once I knew I was free, we were free, but for this girl."

Osprey limped forward and placed a hand on George's shoulder, patting it lovingly. "She will be your countess. It could not be otherwise."

"Why did you never say a word, Osprey?" George wanted to know. "Why did my father keep silent?"

"We keep our ugly, darkest secrets close. We sought redemption for past crimes, our failings, and found it in you. So many, many times your father wanted to share the secrets and lies that brought us to ruin, but I convinced him to say nothing. I feared for your safety. "

"Twice then, we betrayed or insulted Wulfstan of Eskeleth?"

"Not intentionally."

"You betrayed your son Wulfstan to protect me."

"The loss of titles and lands was worth the risk."

"That's what it comes to," George whispered to himself. "Revenge. Everything anyone does is an act of revenge!"

Osprey heard and shook his head, saying, "Love, George. It comes down to love."

"Why didn't you tell me who you were?" George

asked flatly, turning to look up at him. He averted his eyes quickly, avoiding the careful study Osprey was making. Was he hoping to see his daughter, George wondered?

"You would have asked questions, and that would have led to more dangerous questions and confrontation. Is it important now? I think not. What is of great moment is taking this lovely girl home to Grasmere and starting anew. It is something that your father and I wanted for ourselves, but when the time came we squandered our opportunities. Let us celebrate this great victory."

Joanna now stirred and she opened her eyes, first wide with fright and confusion and then softening to contentment when she saw George smiling.

"It's done?" she asked, welcoming his embrace and snuggling close.

"Our friends wait for us – we're going home," George said between kisses and he glanced up at Osprey and nodded.

✠✠✠

THE NEWS OF George's victory reached Grasmere within a day and celebrations were already beginning, with great bonfires lit and its people feasting and drinking as never before. The wastrel good-for-nothing proved himself a good man in most minds and now from Windemere to Keld the people of Cumbria were headed for Skelwith to greet their hero and be a part of the occasion. Whenever a courtier or servant of the castle appeared in the village or on the road they were feted as if George's accomplishment were theirs and cheers went up and bells were rung. But it was quiet at Skelwith as if nothing had happened and it was just another ordinary day, if by ordinary it meant hanging banners and garlands of flowers, and stable boys wearing their best clothes.

"What would you have done, my lord, if the boy hadn't survived?"

Aubrey avoided Maud's question and studied the engraved cup in his grasp; he remembered it as a wedding gift from his parents. He took another drink and set the cup on the table between them. Outside, he could hear the faint cries of the people of Little Langdale as George's caravan approached. Within minutes he would be at Skelwith.

Aubrey poured another cup, but Maud prevented him from taking it as she laid her cold, soft hand on his. He made no effort to move his and said a *pater noster* as he met his wife's exquisitely blue eyes.

"Again I say to you, what would you have done?" she demanded and in the quiet, controlled voice Aubrey always detested.

"More importantly, Maud, he did what better men before him, including me, could not do. That speaks volumes of the Lord working marvelously in our lives," he answered.

"What clever bit of theology would you have tossed out if George were coming home on a funeral bier?"

Again, questions! Why couldn't she be happy for the boy? Aubrey sighed and pulled away from the table, consciously smoothing the fabric of his new habit, feeling the polished wood of the prayer beads that cinched his waistline and brought the soft wool into neat folds around his still-trim soldier's frame. His movements weren't lost on Maud, whose eyes flickered as she watched and just as quickly glanced away to the window. George's pennants and banner were on the horizon.

"If what you want me to say is that I must make amends to the boy, it hasn't been out of mind day or night since I sent him on crusade, and since he returned home an empty shell, and when I forced him to go east," Aubrey said. "When he's settled, we'll talk, and you're welcome to join us."

Maud tapped a finger on the table, the nail clipping beats like a tambor. "Aubrey, I've forgiven you your choice of vocations, but do not think I shall recover soon from what you put our daughter through for him!"

"What word of counsel or comfort did you ever give the boy?" Aubrey snapped. "You gave him no quarter when he returned from Constantinople! You were eager to send him off to Arkengarthdale and out of your sight!"

"And why was it he was so wounded in mind and spirit? Whose fault was that, I wonder? If you had let him go to Rome—"

"Rome! Now there's a place worse than Eskeleth, in my estimation!"

"At least he would have had a better chance of survival."

"My dear, you do not know the world—and you don't know George as well as you thought you knew me. He's as fit for the church as Petronelle to the nunnery! As for his survival in Rome, that is doubtful!" Aubrey sighed as he paced a circle in the bedchamber. "The church is not a cure for all the world's ills—or a man's," he said after a time.

"You're the pot calling the kettle black, my dear!" Maud interjected. "Just why did you leave a comfortable life to cloister yourself if the church is not a salve for wounds?"

"Must we argue about this again, Wife?" He spat the word 'wife' as if it were poison.

"There'll be no peace between us until you explain why you left. I am owed that; do you not think?"

Aubrey turned when he felt her hand on his sleeve, and looked down, seeing his reflection in her eyes. There were tears welling and he used a thumb to gently push aside one drop, letting the thumb trace the outline of her silhouette.

It was a moment before he spoke, for in looking at Maud, he wondered why he had done so many foolish things to hurt her. It was his passion for her that had destroyed two great families and driven him to commit unspeakable things . . .

"Love," he whispered. "I loved you too much to continue failing to be perfect in your sight."

"You thought—!"

"Nothing I ever did seemed to please; or at least I thought so. You thrived without me, and so—"

Maud shook her head and stood on tiptoe to kiss him. The softness of her lips brought back memories of their meeting and bedding at Eskeleth and he wanted to stay in the solar forever, not return to the abbey, but come to the end of time with Maud in his arms.

"My lady?"

Maud spun about and glared at Elinor, who entered the solar and bent in a graceful bow for which

Aubrey gave too much attention.   Monk or no, she thought, glaring at her husband, he was ever the same where it concerned a beautiful girl.

"A door is for knocking upon!" Maud snapped, moving away from Aubrey to neaten her wimple and linen coif.

"Elinor, you look as if it is your wedding day!" Aubrey said with a smile. "And here we thought you were done with George."

"My lord, really . . ." Maud groaned, but hid her delight, seeing the younger woman's discomfort. She'd gladly spend a week on her knees in chapel offering penance for this moment of satisfaction. Elinor wore her finest dress and the most precious of her jewels. Maud didn't think this extra honey would attract George.

"I wish only to honor my lord of Grasmere. We did not part as friends, sir; my lady."

"When did you ever?" Maud purred.

Elinor would have offered a tart reply but the sudden roar of a crowd made them go to the window. George had arrived home.

People crowded on the walkways, parapets and stairwells of the castle between garlands of flowers and bright pennants. More were gathered at the gates to greet George and his sister as they rode up side by side from Little Langdale. The wooden planks and stone walls vibrated with cheers and trumpets sounded as first Petronelle and then George spurred their horses and cantered up and over the drawbridge. As with other homecomings, Maud stood on the donjon steps to welcome her family and their guests, but that evening Aubrey stood with her and it was

Aubrey who came forward first and helped Petronelle from her saddle, and then held her in his arms before releasing her to her mother. The ladies bowed to one another as a matter of formality, but when Petronelle rose, everyone saw the unguarded smile on Maud's lips, and the tears welling in her eyes.

George swung down out of the saddle and took his father's hand in greeting, laughing softly as Aubrey hugged him and called him by a childhood name.

"It's done," George murmured, and reaching out, took the icon from Aubrey's neck and flung it into the moat.

The crowd erupted into more cheering and applause when Joanna rode in, followed by Roger and Adam. George took the reins of her horse and led her to the stairs and helped her down, letting her slide into his arms with a kiss. Petronelle and Maud glanced at Elinor, whose face was frozen in an icy smile.

"They've brought us home safely, my lord," Roger said to Aubrey as he dismounted, and turning to present Adam, added, "Perhaps you know this young lord, Adam Middleton of Gawthorp? The earl of Grasmere has no better a squire and for that we are blessed and grateful."

Aubrey clapped the boy on the shoulders in familiar, brotherly manner, knight to knight, and then turned to George, his brows arched in curiosity, waiting for a formal introduction to the enchanting girl now before them.

"Father, here is Joanna Fletcher," George introduced, bringing her forward, his arm still around her waist. "My worthy second in all things."

Aubrey kissed her hand, saying, "You are blessed, my lady. And we are grateful to you."

Joanna blushed at this and with downcast eyes looked to George, who smiled and nodded. He held out his hand and led her into the donjon.

"You enter as the lady of my heart," George whispered as they went up the staircase and nodded in greeting to the still cheering crowd. He looked over and saw her beguiling smile and the brightness of her eyes.

"How different, my lord, from the first time I entered this great castle," Joanna murmured as she was led forward.

Another feast awaited George and his party, but this time there would be no unwanted guests, nor surprises of the worst kind. While the guests listened to minstrels proclaim the great deeds of the young earl of Grasmere, while they danced and shouted praises for him, George sat quietly, smiling, or staring down at his bowl of wine.

I should be happy; I should be contented; the drum beats and measures whispered.

George watched the happy people of Little Langdale and those who came from Grasmere to celebrate his triumph. Looking down the table, he saw Joanna and raised his cup to her. She nodded and smiled, lifted his ring to her lips and kissed it. Likewise, George drew the crucifix out from under his shirt and held it to his lips for a lingering moment, which made Joanna blush and lower her eyes. All this was not lost on Elinor, sitting to Joanna's right. She smiled prettily and raising her cup in tribute, said, "You needn't prove yourself to me any longer,

George."

"I had no intention, Elinor," he replied and emptied his cup, adding: "And the tribute was not for you."

"No! Peace have done! I've made up my mind!"

The shout stilled the music and conversation. George felt a pang of apprehension, another of dread, and breathed easier. No demons or sorcery, only Petronelle and Chester at the end of the table. It was easy to guess what had happened, especially when Chester glanced over at George and threw him a foul look before storming out.

"Oh dear," Maud sighed.

"Not to worry, Mother; I think there's enough gold in the treasury to mend his broken heart." Offering courtesy, George excused himself from the table and wound through the ribbon of dancers to find some quiet. Both Joanna and Elinor watched him leave and it was Elinor who spoke first. "Have him you may, but not for long!"

"The difference between us, Lady Elinor, is that I expect nothing, and you, everything, including the world," Joanna said. "One's heart isn't about to be broken when little store is put in it. But I suppose wishing him well in any of his endeavors would be too much to ask?"

It was Joanna's turn to offer courtesy and leave.

✠✠✠

THE SUN WAS starting to dip lower on a horizon tinged with saffron and pink washes; motes of light danced on the river sliding under the bridge. George stood there for a moment and listened to the music from the feast while he studied the horizon as if for something particular, he was relieved that he saw nothing in the wisps of clouds overhead nor heard strange messages in the tune to which his family and friends danced.

"I should be happy; I should be contented," he said aloud.

Soon he was walking to the Hiding Place. George threw himself on the soft tufts of grass and leaned back against the tree. Looking around, he half expected to see his father, or even Joanna. They alone seemed to know when he most needed them. When they did not appear, George moved away from the trunk and searched the ground with his fingers. He felt the soft, damp, grass, and then a distinct lump, as if it was a stone. He dug at the soil with a stick until he uncovered and removed a small casket from its own hiding place.

It had been there for years. The catch was rusted, but sprang easily when George flipped the buckle. A scent of earth, wood, leather and roses was released as treasures from childhood were revealed. Searching with a forefinger, George found what he was looking for. A medallion given to him on his twelfth birthday, when the world started turning upside down and his father and mother quarreled day in and day out, and Aubrey was gone for weeks, months, to Lord knew where.

The medallion caught the last rays of sunlight and highlighted the relief of Saint Michael in a contest with the Devil. George now knew why it had been gifted. Why Aubrey had been gone for weeks and months, to Lord knew where.

One question still remained unanswered.

Putting his head in his hands, George sighed painfully. "What do I do, Lord?" he moaned.

A rustle of leaves and a soft scuff on the ground made George look around the tree trunk.

"What do you want to do, George?" Joanna asked softly, kneeling beside him.

George kissed the palm cupping his cheek so lovingly and pulled her into his arms to kiss her mouth.

"Have they sent you to fetch me back?" George chuckled and was relieved when she shook her head and kissed his brow, then his eyelids, then his nose and offered the most passionate yet chaste kiss he had yet experienced. It aroused him so that he tumbled her gently onto the grass and was grateful she was receptive to his idea of lovemaking under a canopy of twilight stars and the boughs of a lone tree.

"I love you!" George whispered as they said good night at the donjon steps and the bells rang midnight. He slipped the Archangel's medallion around her neck and gave her a lingering kiss before she slipped inside.

Most but not all of the guests had either gone home or to their beds in the castle living quarters and George was relieved to not have to face questioning eyes or knowing smiles until he crossed the great hall, stepping over retainers and knights bedding down in corners, and found Roger alone on the stairs to the lady tower, drinking long and deep from a wineskin.

"Good night for a walk," Roger greeted, passing the wineskin, and with a tilt of his head towards the living quarters, added, "or a bit of lovemaking with a pretty girl."

"We had left things unresolved," muttered George, sitting beside him.

"Resolution is a good thing. How is our dragonslayer this evening?"

"The ancient legends never mention what the hero does after he slays the dragon, after the cheers fade, the guests are drunk, the girl slips away after a badly managed tryst, and he's left to himself," said George, offering the wineskin back.

"What do you want to do?"

"Drink."

"Good night to get drunk, then." Roger said, and handing over the wineskin again, added, "We'll have to find another."

Which they did in the kitchens. Servants went about their work of cleaning up after the feast while the two young men sat at a table and shared a jug.

"What will you do now?" George yawned, staring into his cup and frowning when he saw it was empty.

"I ride for Gawthorp in the morning—I'm taking Adam home, and then I'll speak with his mother about his education; one way or another I'll make him a knight."

"He'll have to learn to use his sword rather than his mouth."

"His tongue is sharper than any weapon I've held. My work will not be easy. Then I must continue on to London."

"What's in London?"

"My mother. I intend to marry, so I want her blessing."

George nodded. "I'm surprised; you never said a word of it to me. What did my sister say when you told her the news?"

"She said yes. It surprised us both, but after all that's happened…"

Roger started to laugh when he saw George's face and harder still when the last of wine was sputtered over the table and floor and George coughed to keep from choking.

"Roger!" George laughed when he caught his breath. "Do you know what you're getting yourself into?"

"I do hope so—and I could do with the loan of three hundred sovereigns; it was the most I could come up with to buy off Chester and prevent him from taking action against you for breach of contract!"

"I'll make a wedding present of twice the dower," George said, clapping him on the back. "It seems that I am only out gold, but you're paying with your life!"

"A small sacrifice for happiness, George. A very little thing, in truth."

"Happiness is no small thing," George murmured.

No, it wasn't, he thought an hour later while he still sat in the kitchen. Roger had gone up to bed whistling a tune they'd heard in Constantinople. Expecting a pang of shock or remorse, George was relieved when all he felt was tired and drunk. In this state he rode to Grasmere and to the abbey. Brother Porter raised his brows when he saw who rang the bell. "Do you seek sanctuary, my lord?" he asked.

"I seek an audience with my father if he is not abed and will see me."

No further persuasion was needed and George

was led to the abbot's lodgings where he took a bench in the private chapel and waited only a moment for Aubrey. George stood upon his father's entrance and knelt for a blessing, which was given. When he stood, Aubrey looked up, searching his son's eyes for an indication of what was amiss.

"We never had a chance to talk," George said when Aubrey finally asked. "I feel like one of the disciples on the road to Emmaus," George commented in jest as they sat on a bench along the wall. "I cannot see my salvation, though it is right before me, and has been all along." He turned to look at his father and smiled sadly. "Were you never going to tell me that you and Wulfstan's sister were lovers?"

Aubrey expelled a painful sigh. "Yes, in time."

"And that she was my mother?"

"In time."

"A lot of bitter medicine to take all at once, Father."

"We were betrothed to settle a quarrel between Ascalon and Eskeleth over lands and a castle. My father made incursions into Arkengarthdale to seek vengeance for the death of his brother at the hands of Wulfstan. One thing led to another – you know how it is. Thus a marriage was arranged to keep the peace," Aubrey said. He leaned against the wall and sighed. "So long ago, it was. I didn't want the marriage – what man does when being offered up as a sacrifice? I wasn't getting a shire or farm for my part in it. Not even a war horse, or armor. But then I saw my betrothed and I wanted her as I wanted no other woman."

"One thing led to another," George said half in

jest. "The inevitable, I suppose?"

"Those were sweet nights and days," Aubrey murmured. "When I discovered what was expected of me and the price of the marriage, I couldn't go through with it. It didn't help that the lady revealed her true self, a dark and unhappy woman bent on having her way in all things and as unforgiving as iron is hard—besides, I'd seen a girl who took my breath away."

"Mother."

"I made two pledges in my life, and I've kept two of them—the first to Maud, the second to God. I thought I would be contented, living a quiet life as a nobleman, looking after my lands and revenues, answering summons to court. Like you, George, I was haunted by things done and left undone. And so I had to honor a pledge, and in doing so, I was compelled to honor the most important and singular pledge. We tried to speak of it but it never ended peacefully. So one morning after you'd left for crusade I rose from our bed, kissed her while she slept, and I left at dawn. I doubt if she'll ever forgive me. I have wronged her, you know."

"I forgive you, Father!"

George leaned over and embraced him, held his father for the longest time and when he felt the dampness of tears on his neck, he pushed away self-consciously. Without a word, George hurried out of the chapel, not wishing to see his father weep.

Or Aubrey to see his own tears.

CHAPTER 20

S ERVANTS WERE CLEANING up the remains of the banquet when George returned, side-stepping the hounds foraging for leftovers in the rushes and guests who had fallen asleep or passed out at the tables.

"The lady countess has gone to bed, as have all the others," William Longleate answered George's inquiry as to the whereabouts of his family.

George took the staircase to the living quarters on the third floor and found Joanna's chamber. He entered quietly and sat by the bed where she was curled up amongst plump pillows, fur-lined coverlets, and linen sheets, looking very young and very small. He touched her cheek with a finger, lovingly moving aside the strands of hair that shifted with her exhaled breaths. She stirred and sat up, surprised to find him there, self-conscious about her appearance.

"I'm like a stray puppy," he greeted.

"My lord—George . . ."

"How fares my lady?" George greeted, offering a kiss.

"Come, sir," Joanna whispered, shifting the blankets. He kicked off his boots and slid into bed beside her, laying his head on her breast.

"You look like one who has something to confess," she murmured into his hair. "Is there a serving girl I should know about?"

"No!" George exclaimed, sitting up. She laughed softly and pulled him down, wrapping him in her arms. "It takes getting used to, being home."

"It takes getting used to knowing one has a home. Thank you for that, George."

They settled in and slept in each other's arms as they had in the pavilion at Eskeleth, waking at first light. George rose first and splashed water on his face, letting the chill shock him awake. He waited as the servants dressed Joanna and led her to the countess's apartments. "Wait here," he said to Joanna, and kissed her before entering the solar.

Maud looked up from her usual place at the window, closing the Bible gently and nodding to George as he approached and knelt before her chair.

"Good morning, Madam," he greeted, kissing her hand. "I have news I think you will be glad of. I've found a wife."

It took a moment for Maud to consider what he'd said and then she smiled. "Why, this is good news indeed! But George, when did you have time? Perhaps the daughter of an Outremer lord, or—"

"She is the daughter of the earl of Merioneth and her name is Joan ap Elen. And you are well acquainted, I think."

George nodded to the footman, who opened the door so that Joanna might enter. She smiled shyly and bowed before Maud, keeping her eyes downcast—if anything, to avoid the look of horror that colored the countess's face.

"The leman from Butcher's Lane?" Maud hissed, rising to her feet.

"She is Joan ap Elen, called Joanna, the daughter of—"

"That's as you say!" Maud spat, turning to Joanna, who trembled and fell to her knees.

"That was her misfortune to be turned out because of her father's actions," George said quietly.

"You would have the daughter of an attainted lord? An enemy of the king?"

"The leman from Butcher's Lane is what you first said. What's it to be, Mother? Pardon, I beg you, but it seems you're not my mother, and that makes your disapproval of my wife all the more curious to me — or do you prefer to keep up the ruse?"

Maud swung at him and George caught the hand before it struck his cheek.

"Now it is perfectly clear why you treated me with little more than indifference," George said quietly.

"Now we may speak freely and have it all in the open, is that what you truly mean? To humiliate and shame your sister and me?"

"Is that what you think I want?" George asked, astonished. "All I ever wanted was your love. It was too much to ask." He rose and brought Joanna with him. "We shall be married. Be glad for us."

Saying this, George swept out of the solar with Joanna, banging the doors shut. Maud toyed with the prayer beads in her lap and then turned to the page she'd left open in the Bible. The words of the prophet Sirach lay before her:

> *. . . It is heartache and sorrow when a wife is jealous of a rival, and a tongue-lashing makes it known to all. A bad wife is a chafing yoke; taking hold of her is like*

grasping a scorpion.

Maud sighed. And here she thought she'd always been the obedient and loyal partner to Aubrey.

That still must appear to be so, she thought. That still must appear to be so, even if she would have to act to save herself and her daughter. . .

CHAPTER 21

THE ASCALON FAMILY, their friends and
retainers were gathered for Petronelle's
wedding feast in the gardens at Skelwith, the
day being unseasonably warm and the skies clear, with
no threat of rain. George drank to the health of his
sister and brother-in-law; danced with the women;
and shared stories with Adam, who had come from
Gawthorp with his mother and brother for the
occasion.

"If all these ladies were dancing in their shifts or
less, you'd still have eyes for only one girl," Adam
teased George, who was watching Joanna dance with
Roger.

"When is the wedding, George?" Lady Middleton
teased.

"In August at the abbey church in Grasmere.
Perhaps you will lodge with us until that time, Lady
Middleton? It's not that far off."

"Do not tempt me, sir! I could grow fond of
Ascalon's hospitality and the lord of Grasmere," the
woman tittered.

George winked and set his cup down. "Alas, I am
already spoken for," he sighed, and they laughed
together. "But we may at least dance."

Standing, he offered his hand, and Lady
Middleton simpered and giggled as she was led to the

dancing pavilion. He glided easily to the musician's strains until the measure, when they exchanged partners, and George found himself partnering Maud.

"The Lord and Lady of Osterle and Kenning, Count and Countess of Myrce," George remarked as they crossed paths with Petronelle and Roger. "Be glad for them, Mother. Roger is worth twenty of Chester."

"He will not have to petition the king to keep what is his," Maud commented, "nor place his entire family in peril."

"I doubt there will be any quarrel with King John, nor shall we have cause to worry. I've already sent a man to London to argue our case. Joanna will be once again heiress to the Merioneth lands and revenues, the richest entitlement of Wales. She is the only living heir to her father and stands to inherit all," George explained as they weaved in and out of couples while pipes and drums played.

"And what do you want from me? You've made up your mind to do as you please!" Maud whispered angrily as the dance ended.

"Your approval, I suppose. I have Father's,"

"That is no surprise. You don't need mine."

"I want my mother's approval. You're the only mother I've known."

"I'd sooner you go to Jerusalem. Become a Templar as you promised, and then we will have something to talk about."

"Out of sight, out of mind? Locked up in a monastery in Jerusalem where I'd be forgotten, rather than marry and get sons to remind you of Father's weakness and betrayal."

"A blemish is best covered!"

George studied Maud's beautiful face, the perfect oval eyes and mouth, and shook his head. "I will be a faithful and loving husband to my wife. My sons will not have to pay for my sins and missteps. Tell me if there was ever a moment, any insignificant time, when you had regard for me. If you won't give me your blessing, then answer me that. It isn't much and it's all I ask—and I'll trouble you no more."

It must appear to be so . . .

The thought came to Maud suddenly like the sharp pain of a pin prick, remembering her promise to God of weeks past. She burned with a bright color of shame on her cheeks, realizing her sins of jealousy and pride.

She looked up at him, saying, "Then you have my blessing if that's all you want, George."

He considered her for a moment. "I want to believe you."

When the music died, George held out his hand for Joanna, bringing her to a quiet corner of the garden that faced the river, where the roses bloomed and their perfume reminded George of the secret garden at Eskeleth.

Joanna needed no prompting to kiss him, for over the weeks, they had eased into the warm familiarity of lovers. She curled up next to him, one hand on the ring and medallion around her neck.

"Next month, is it?" she murmured.

"If you would still have it so."

"I do, George. The tone of your voice makes me think you do not."

"It's something my mother said. She'd rather I

keep my pledge and go to Jerusalem. Profess the life of a Templar."

"If you did that we'd never be able speak to one another again, nor even touch. Tell me you're not thinking —?" The anxiety in Joanna's voice, the darkness of her eyes betrayed the quiet tone.

"I don't know what to think, Love. I know what is expected of me,"

"Haven't you already done what is expected of you? Is it not time for you to pursue that which you want?"

"It's come down to the matter of what I want – and I don't know what that is."

"You once asked me what becomes of a knight who has neither heart nor mind for the pursuits of nobility."

"That I did."

"He grows wheat to make bread," Joanna replied. "But truly, is that all he wants?"

"I don't know. I need time to think. Joanna, I need time to think of all that has been, all that may or will be. I've been thinking about something the apostle Paul wrote. Some of the words were engraved on the fuller of my sword. 'The night is far gone, the day is near. Let us then lay aside the works of darkness and put on the armor of light.' I've done that. I've stopped having nightmares about Constantinople—and about Eskeleth. Where once I dreamed of war, of fighting, of soldiers, now I dream of quiet presence, of stillness, of a heartbeat measured in cadence with mine."

"I'll give you all that for a wedding gift."

"Joanna! Joan, are you saying–?"

"I am saying that you know I am not obedient, but I am patient."

"I love you!"

"Now you must do it, and we must make plans," Joanna whispered, turning in his arms for a kiss.

✠✠✠

WHAT A SPLENDID assembly, George thought, smiling, as he stood at the entrance to the nave and waited a moment before entering with Adam, taking his place at the steps of the sanctuary before the Bishop of Cumbria. The doors to the church were kept open and the scent of high summer—roses, bluebells, and the lake—wafted in with a breeze that danced with the hems of finely made gowns and diaphanous veils, made the candle flames bow and sway, and cast wavering shadows with the setting sun.

Gasps of approval and awe behind him told George that Joanna had entered the church on Roger's arm. He turned then, extending his hand to his bride, who was dressed in pale blue and silver silk and velvet, a silver mantle across her shoulders and a coronet of sapphires securing her veil. They smiled at one another and knelt before the bishop.

The choir began to sing and when the last notes drifted away, the bishop nodded to George, who unsheathed his sword and laid it at his feet.

"Here I do renounce my worldly titles and lands, and all appurtenances thereto, offering myself to God as His servant, for as long as He would have it," George pronounced in a clear, confident voice.

The delighted whispers making the rounds of the nave now became agitated questions. The wedding guests began to talk amongst themselves and watched as George knelt and placed his hands between those of the bishop. Only his family sat quietly in stunned silence.

"It is agreed, George Ascalon, that you shall present yourself to the abbey tomorrow and relinquish your armor and all symbols of your knighthood?" the bishop asked.

"It shall be so," George answered.

"And do you swear to uphold the rights of your wife, the countess Joanna, whom you wed yester evening?"

More gasps filled the nave. George waited a moment and said, looking at her, "I so swear before God, before you, my lord, and my wife, that all I have is hers by right. I leave her in your protection."

He rose, bringing Joanna with him, and accepted the sword of Ascalon back from the bishop's hands. After a blessing George and Joanna followed him out of the church.

"Let us say good bye properly, then?" she whispered, meeting his smile with one of her own.

"What have you done? What have you done? I demand to know! Tell me!" Petronelle shouted over the rising protests and commentary. She might have gone after them, but Aubrey held her back.

"Joanna will speak with you in the morning. They need some time together."

Only Maud seemed unperturbed by the change of events. While everyone filed out of the church she alone stayed behind and when everyone was gone, knelt in thanksgiving before the statue of the Virgin and Child. Perhaps it would not be so difficult after all to make all appear as it should, make it be as it should.

✠✠✠

THE TIME WAS brief, but at sunrise the next day, Joanna watched as George put on the ordinary clothes of a plain solider and then like an experienced groom she dressed him in his armor. The sword of Ascalon stood in its usual place by the bed, leaning up against the chests the mattress sat on. Joanna took it and studied the outline of the worn letters on the fuller.

"We shall have to give you a new sword," she said. "It is the custom for the bride's family to give the husband a new sword."

"I want no other – and no other wife."

Feeling the sting of tears, Joanna quietly and carefully placed the sword in its scabbard on George's belt, stood back as he set a coronet on his head and kicked the worn and faded tabard of a crusader under the bed.

"Do I look the part?" he asked with a ragged sigh.

"Like Saint Michael," she murmured smiling, wiping her cheeks with the back of a hand.

"I'll stay if you like."

"No," Joanna whispered, kissing him. "You made a promise and must go."

"I'll go quietly, then, before the household is up and questions are asked. It's what the earls of Grasmere do best."

Joanna saw him to the stable yard where he took one of the roan mares and walked with it and Joanna to the drawbridge. After a long, lingering kiss and embrace, they watched as the bridge came down, and Joanna watched George ride out of the castle towards

Grasmere, to the abbey.

Joanna returned to their bedchamber in Ravenglass Tower and picked up his clothes and effects as any wife might, tidying the bed that was still warm from their lovemaking.

She was a wife; she was a lady in waiting.

Time would tell how long before his return. Joanna had learned that life could take so many different journeys, and they all ended before God.

Sighing, she smiled as she pulled the crusader's tabard out from under the bed and brought it with her to the window seat overlooking Little Langdale and the Hiding Place. From around her neck, she took the ring and broke the ribbon. The ring she placed on the third finger of her left hand, the ribbon she tied around her wrist. Lastly, she caught up the puppy and let it lap her face with kisses.

There she sat and watched the morning colors change with the rising sun, her hand resting lightly against her body where she was sure their child lay.

PAX ET BONUM

ACKNOWLEDGMENTS

"Write a story that you want to tell, but don't use someone else's words and tell a story already written." That was the advice from my college English Lit professor, and two days later, I received a brochure from a famous New York literary agency for the time. I can't remember the professor or the agency's names, but I remember the advice and often share it, in my own words, with aspiring novelists. My thanks to all those who encouraged me, especially with this, my third novel.

Ellen L. Ekstrom is a native of the San Francisco Bay Area and was educated locally. She holds a bachelor's degree in theological studies and her area of concentration is Christian Mythos, also known as church history, with a sub-specialty in Christian Social Ethics, for both of which she took honors. Ellen has been fascinated by all things medieval since childhood and is now studying Late Anglo-Saxon England in preparation for two forthcoming novels, *Swannsaeld,* and *The Sometime Queen.*

The genres Ellen prefers to work in are fantasy/historical: her first novel was *The Legacy,* a tale of fourteenth-century Florence and Tuscany, followed by her retelling of the St. George and the Dragon legend, *Armor of Light,* and *St. Edmund Wood,* a story of Victorian England. Once in a while, she delves into matters of the modern heart, as evidenced by her novels in the *Midwinter Sonata* series and *What She Wished For… a Cautionary Tale.* Just as a painter has many subjects to bring to a canvas, Ellen believes that there are many stories to tell and to limit oneself to a niche isn't the way she lives and thinks.